Down, girl.

Rachel stared at a man in jeans and work shirt coming down the stairs. He was about thirty-three and darkly handsome, with what looked like several drops of Native American blood in his veins. He was a good six foot two with broad shoulders, working man's hands and startling brown eyes that, despite her better instincts, made Rachel's heart stutter.

"There's nothing going on that a little tried-and-true police work won't fix." He held out a hand. "I'm Nick Chavaree, the local sheriff. I'm staying here while my house is being..." He paused, frowned, withdrew the hand. "You look familiar to me. Do I know you?"

Rachel was pretty sure that if she'd seen him before she'd remember. He was *that* good-looking. "No, I don't think so."

His demeanor abruptly shifted from friendly to hostile. "You're here about the murders, aren't you?"

"Murders?"

"Don't be coy." He moved toward her now. "That's why you picked this place to stay. You thought you could get some inside information from me. That's not going to happen."

ALANA MATTHEWS

WATERFORD POINT

TORONTO NEW YORK LONDON
AMSTERDAM PARIS SYDNEY HAMBURG
STOCKHOLM ATHENS TOKYO MILAN MADRID
PRAGUE WARSAW BUDAPEST AUCKLAND

Recycling programs
for this product may
not exist in your area.

ISBN-13: 978-0-373-69538-6

WATERFORD POINT

Copyright © 2011 by Alana Matthews

ABOUT THE AUTHOR

Alana Matthews can't remember a time when she didn't want to be a writer. As a child, she was a permanent fixture in her local library, and she soon turned her passion for books into writing short stories, and finally novels. A longtime fan of romantic suspense, Alana felt she had no choice but to try her hand at the genre, and she is thrilled to be writing for Harlequin Intrigue. Alana makes her home in a small town near the coast of Southern California, where she spends her time writing, composing music and watching her favorite movies.

Send a message to Alana at her website, www.AlanaMatthews.com.

Books by Alana Matthews

HARLEQUIN INTRIGUE
1208—MAN UNDERCOVER
1239—BODY ARMOR
1271—WATERFORD POINT

CAST OF CHARACTERS

Rachel Hudson—She came to Waterford Point to escape her past, and found herself caught up in someone else's.

Sheriff Nick Chavaree—A puzzling murder investigation threatened his career, but could Rachel help him ferret out the truth...and steal his heart?

Maddie—She kept herself busy running the Waterford Inn, but what dark secret was she hiding?

Deputy Charlie Tevis—He returned to Waterford Point after an extended absence and wondered if he should have stayed away.

Mayor Bill Burgess—An officious fool who was more concerned about Waterford Point's tourist trade than its own citizens.

Caroline Keller—The first in a string of murder victims who heard someone crying in the night.

Weeping Willow—Did her spirit come back to Waterford Point looking for revenge?

Prologue

The crying was what awakened her.

For a moment she thought she was dreaming; the sound circled inside her head like a persistent insect, refusing to go away. But as she fully awakened, she realized that it was all too real, a muffled but unmistakable keen coming from outside her bedroom window.

She abruptly pulled herself upright and strained to hear, a vague uneasiness simmering in her chest.

Was it an animal of some kind? A bird? An injured deer?

No.

This was definitely human.

And female.

Feeling a knot in her stomach, she swung her legs around and stood, surprised by the chill of the polished wooden floorboards beneath her bare feet.

This wasn't her first night here, and she knew

she should be used to her surroundings by now. But it seemed that every time she got out of bed, she anticipated the feel of warm carpet—the carpet in her own bedroom in D.C.—only to be startled by this cold bare floor.

Padding to the window, she undid the latch and pushed it open, letting in the night air. The sound floated in just beneath the whisper of the wind—

The sobs of a broken girl.

A soul irrevocably wounded.

It came from a forest of Eastern pine that stood just forty yards away from the old house, across a rustic backyard. A thin mist hung in the air around the trees, the forest dark and foreboding.

Her heart thumped wildly as she listened to the sobs, and with sudden dread she knew she'd made a mistake coming home again.

The stories she'd heard were true.

This wasn't make-believe. A fairy tale. A quaint little piece of local folklore. And as much as she might try, she knew she'd never be rid of her past.

It was right outside.

Haunting her.

Waiting for her in the trees.

Chapter One

By the time the ferry reached the dock, Rachel Hudson was a little queasy.

She didn't travel well on water. Although the trip across the bay hadn't taken more than fifteen minutes, her stomach wasn't exactly rock solid these days, and she thought for a moment she might lose the salad she'd had for lunch.

Thank God for dry land.

Rachel had never been to Waterford Point before. Had never been to Penobscot Bay or farther north than Connecticut, for that matter. But the photos she'd seen on the internet had convinced her that this was where she needed to go. That Waterford Point was *exactly* the place she should be right now.

Her means of escape.

Her bastion of refuge.

An isolated fishing village-cum-tourist destination on an island off the coast of Maine, it was a place where she could forget about the chaos that had swirled around her in California and finally decide what to do with her life now that Dan was officially out of the picture.

As the ferry gate opened, she moved with the handful of homeward-bound commuters and rolled her suitcase onto the dock, looking out toward the village.

It was quite a bit larger than she had anticipated and she wasn't sure she wanted to spend her next few weeks here getting around on foot.

As the others moved toward their cars in the parking lot, Rachel turned to the dockworker who was manning the gate. He was an elderly man with a weathered, sunbaked face, and she had no doubt that he'd spent many years on a fishing boat.

"Is there a place around here I can rent a car?"

"Yes, ma'am." He pointed toward a cluster of wooden shacks to the right of the dock. "They're on the far side of that last building, just around the corner. You can't miss 'em. And they'll be glad to see you, too."

"Oh? Why's that?"

"Not too many visitors around here lately, what with all the commotion."

"Commotion?"

He shook his head then; he'd said too much.

"Nothing to be concerned about. You just enjoy yourself and be sure to spend lots of money."

He grinned, and Rachel felt compelled to push him further, but she resisted the urge.

She had come here to get her head together, not work. Work was the last thing she needed to be thinking about.

THE CAR RENTAL AGENCY was an eight-by-ten office with an efficient-looking beanpole of a kid manning the counter.

The old guy at the dock had been right. Rachel's arrival seemed to be the high point of this young man's evening, and he cheerfully rented her a Ford compact, which was parked along the side of the building amidst a couple dozen identical cars.

Despite his cheerfulness, there was something off about the kid's demeanor. A nervousness behind the smile. He was trying too hard, Rachel thought, and she again found herself feeling the urge to ask about it.

But again she resisted.

He wasn't a witness to a crime, or a convict staring out from behind a Plexiglas wall. He was an overly enthusiastic rental clerk and she was letting her natural curiosity get the better of her. What was going on inside his head was really none of her business.

She needed to relax and forget who and what she was for a while.

For the sake of the baby, if nothing else.

RACHEL'S PREGNANCY had come as a complete shock.

One night of mechanical sex—*protected* sex at that—did not often have such stupefying consequences, and while bearing a child was something she had dreamed of for many years, she'd always shoved the thought aside in favor of her career.

But now that motherhood would soon be a reality, Rachel was overjoyed.

Unfortunately, Dan hadn't shared in that joy.

"You're *what?*" he'd said when she broke the news to him.

She had asked to meet him for dinner, but he'd opted for a cup of coffee instead. An entire meal was too much of a commitment.

They sat in a trendy roasting house in Hollywood on a busy Tuesday afternoon and despite the lunchtime chatter around them, Dan's voice cut straight through and hit her right in the gut.

"Pregnant," she repeated, feeling annoyed by his reaction. "You want me to spell it for you?"

But just as he'd made it clear that he no longer loved her, Dan made it equally clear that he had no interest whatsoever in being a father, and had flat-out refused to believe that it was *his* child growing inside her.

Rachel knew, of course, that the baby didn't belong to anyone else. She hadn't slept with another man since the divorce, hadn't even *dated,* for godsakes.

So whether he liked the idea or not, Dan was indeed the father.

She could easily convince him with a paternity test, but what was the point? If he had no interest in loving and caring for their child, no blood test in the world would change his mind.

Or, more importantly, his heart.

So she knew she was on her own. Not an ideal situation emotionally, but she was fairly thick-skinned and she'd done well enough in her profession not to have to worry about income for several years.

And while raising a child alone was not something she was thrilled about, she knew she could manage. Even if it meant putting her work on hold for a while.

Still, Rachel couldn't help feeling a little lost and lonely, and she sometimes wished she had a partner to share this joy with. A man who would love her, unconditionally, and welcome her child into the world with open arms.

Good luck with that one.

THE DRIVE TO THE WATERFORD Inn took her less than ten minutes.

A large, refurbished Victorian, it stood at the end of a long block that was bordered by a hillside studded with trees. It was late in the day, and everywhere Rachel looked, those trees seemed to be shrouded in mist.

Hopefully tomorrow would bring some sunshine.

The house itself stood in stark contrast, its freshly painted pastel-blue both homey and inviting. But as she stepped out of the car and locked her door, Rachel didn't feel welcome at all.

Sensing someone watching her, she turned to find two women staring at her from across the road as they walked together toward the center of town.

There was mistrust in their expressions, a look that made her feel instantly uneasy. Was this simply the usual locals-versus-tourist hostility, or something else altogether?

To Rachel's mind it looked more like suspicion.

Or even *fear*.

The two women looked away from her now, chattering quietly as they walked. She had no idea what they were saying and didn't really want to know.

It couldn't be anything good.

Ignoring them, she took her suitcase from the trunk and moved up the front steps of the inn.

A moment later she was inside a quaint, old-fashioned foyer with a small reception counter on one side and shelves full of books on the other. Beyond, through a wide doorway, was a dining parlor and a polished wooden staircase that led to the second floor.

Rachel heard a faint grunt and moved up to the counter. A woman in her mid-forties was crouched behind it, searching through a low drawer, all of her concentration centered on the task.

Rachel cleared her throat and the woman jerked her head up and sucked in a breath, touching her chest in surprise.

"Oh, my," she said. "You scared the bojangles out of me."

Rachel offered her a sympathetic smile. "I was hoping you heard me come in."

"I can't hear a thing when I'm concentrating." She gestured to the open drawer. "And I can't seem to find my scissors, either. You wouldn't happen to have a pair on you, would you?"

Rachel shook her head and smiled. "The one thing I forgot to pack."

"I don't know where they got to. Maybe in back, by my bed. I don't like to sleep without some kind of…" She glanced at Rachel's suitcase and frowned. "Who exactly *are* you?"

It was Rachel's turn to be surprised. "Rachel… Rachel Hudson. I have a reservation?"

The woman took a moment to make the connection, then raised her eyebrows. "You didn't get my message?"

"Message?"

"I told you not to bother coming, dearie. We're not taking in guests for a while."

"What? Why?"

The woman was about to respond when her gaze shifted to a spot behind the counter. "*There* they are!"

She reached forward and brought out a pair of sharp sewing shears.

"I didn't get any message," Rachel said. "And I need a place to stay."

The woman was holding the shears just below the handle now, her fingers wrapped around it as if it were a dagger. She made several practice stabbing motions in the air, her eyes fixed on the blades. She seemed to have forgotten about Rachel altogether.

"Hello?"

The woman looked up sharply. "I know you came a long way," she said, sounding only slightly apologetic, "but if you had any sense in you, you'd turn around right now and go back home."

"Why?"

She lowered the scissors and leaned forward, gesturing for Rachel to come close.

Rachel hesitated, not sure the woman was all there. Then she did as she was asked and the woman whispered, "It's for your own good, my dear. This place isn't safe. She won't rest until we're all dead."

Rachel was confused. "She?"

The woman straightened again, forgetting all about the apparent need to whisper. "You haven't heard about her?"

"Who?"

"Weeping Willow, that's—"

"All right, Maddie, enough."

Rachel turned to find a guy in jeans and a work shirt coming down the stairs. He was about thirty-three and darkly handsome, with what looked like several drops of Native American blood in his veins. He was a good six foot two with broad shoulders, workingman's hands and startling brown eyes that, despite her better instincts, made Rachel's heart stutter.

Down, girl.

"Quit scaring the guests," he said to Maddie. "How

do you expect to make a living, chasing people away all the time?"

"She needs to know what's going on around here."

"There's nothing going on that a little tried-and-true police work won't fix." He held out a hand for Rachel to shake. "I'm Nick Chavaree, the local sheriff. I'm staying here while my house is being…" He paused, frowned, withdrew the hand. "You look familiar to me. Do I know you?"

Rachel was pretty sure that if she'd seen him before she'd remember. He was *that* good-looking. "No, I don't think so."

"Wait," he said, then crossed to the bookshelves. He searched for a moment, then pulled down a worn paperback that Rachel knew all too well.

A Dangerous Mind.

Her first bestseller.

Flipping the book over, Chavaree studied the photo on the back—an old one that needed to be updated—then looked at Rachel. "Tell me this isn't you."

"Sometimes I wish I could."

Even after three books in the top ten, she still wasn't used to being recognized. Most writers remain anonymous their entire lives. But she'd spent enough time on the cable networks and the morning talk shows to become something of a celebrity.

She half expected Chavaree to ask her to sign the book, but his demeanor abruptly shifted from friendly to hostile. "You're here about the murders, aren't you?"

"Murders?"

"Don't be coy." He moved toward her now. "That's why you picked this place to stay. You thought you could get some inside information from me."

She had no earthly idea what he was talking about, but had a feeling it explained a lot. These murders obviously had something to do with the so-called "commotion"—and probably the looks she'd gotten outside—but she wasn't interested in finding out.

"I'm just here for a little rest and relaxation," she said. "Nothing more."

"Uh-huh." Not bothering to hide his skepticism, Chavaree tossed the book on the counter, then took a jacket out of the closet. "I admire your talent, Ms. Hudson. Your books are always compelling. But I'm gonna say this just once, okay?"

Rachel frowned. "Okay…"

"You're not wanted here. I've got enough problems to handle without you sticking your nose in where it doesn't belong."

"I just *told* you, I'm here for a vaca—"

"Don't even bother," he said, then yanked his jacket on and went outside.

Chapter Two

People were often surprised when they found out what Rachel did for a living. There were dozens of successful crime writers in the world, but, with a few notable exceptions, most of them were men.

Rachel was one of those exceptions.

She had begun her career fresh out of college, after realizing that she was no longer interested in following in her father's footsteps. Despite all the courses she'd taken in criminology and forensics, working for the LAPD didn't really appeal to her.

Her passion lay in *writing* about crime. She was fascinated by the motives that lay behind the violence, the emotional histories, the family stories, the sometimes petty insecurities that led people to strike out against their fellow human beings.

All of these things factored into any good homicide investigation, but in the end, the work her father did came down to a simple who-did-what-to-whom, and Rachel knew that filing a few police reports would not lead her to a fulfilling life. Neither would walking a beat for several years just to get her detective's shield.

So, much to her father's disappointment, she worked as a crime reporter for a small daily newspaper in the Valley. Thanks to her college coursework and her father's willingness to teach her the ins and outs of homicide investigation, she had adapted to the job quickly, soon moving on to the *Los Angeles Tribune,* then to the world of true crime books.

Her stories of murder and mayhem and family connections gone wrong now lined the shelves of libraries and bookstores around the world.

The only drawback was immersing herself in the darkest side of human nature. She heard stories told by cold, heartless men and women that would send chills up the spines of most people, and had been forced to find a way to distance herself from the horror. In the process she'd become desensitized to the violence. She was sure that this had contributed to her failures with Dan.

How could it not?

But Rachel hadn't come to Waterford Point in search of a story. In fact, it was just the opposite; she had too many things weighing on her brain right now to be concerned with a couple of small-town murders.

After Chavaree left, she stewed for a moment, thinking she'd like to chase after him and give him a piece of her mind for being so rudely presumptuous. But when she thought about it, she really couldn't blame him. *She* probably wouldn't have believed her, either.

Instead, she spent the next several minutes trying to convince Maddie to give her a room.

"I paid a deposit," she said. "I made a reservation. In my world that's a contract."

Maddie took the book from the countertop and looked it over. "In your world, huh? Out there in Hollywood?"

"And right here in Waterford Point, too. Murders or no murders."

Maddie squinted at her. "Were you telling Nick the truth? Are you really here for a vacation or are you trying to pull a sly one on him, get close to his investigation?"

"I couldn't care less about his investigation. I have my own problems to work out." She gestured toward the stairs. "I've had a long trip and I'm tired. Are you going to give me a room or not?"

Maddie studied her a moment. "You're a stubborn

one, I'll give you that. You sure you aren't worried about the ghost?"

This threw Rachel for a loop. "Ghost?"

Her utter perplexity must have shown, because Maddie softened and said, "Child, you really *don't* know anything, do you?"

"Haven't I been saying that all along?"

RACHEL WASN'T SURE when exactly she'd made the breakthrough, but Maddie started searching again and brought out a key.

Relieved, Rachel reached for her suitcase, but the woman quickly came around the counter and grabbed it.

"Someone in your condition shouldn't be lifting," she said.

Rachel was only four months pregnant and while she'd certainly grown thicker around the middle, she had no idea she was showing. "Is it that obvious?"

"To the trained eye, it is. I used to work for an obstetrician over in Rockland. Only came back here to Waterford after my folks passed away."

"I'm sorry to hear that. Did they own this place?"

"They did, indeed. In fact, the room you'll be sleeping in used to be theirs."

They climbed the stairs. Maddie struggled slightly

with the suitcase, and Rachel felt a twinge of guilt. She was perfectly capable of carrying the thing herself, but she knew Maddie was not the kind of woman to be trifled with, and let her have her way.

"Breakfast every morning at 8:00 a.m.," Maddie said. "No stragglers. Nothing I hate worse than serving cold eggs."

"Okay. No straggling."

"Nick's the only other guest we have right now, and you'll have to share a bathroom with him. He's a man, and men are messy, but he does his best and I do what I can to clean up after him."

Rachel's own bathroom back home had clothes piled on the floor and a counter that looked like a beauty salon after a hurricane. Messy wasn't something she was particularly concerned with.

When they reached the top of the stairs, Maddie turned to her.

"You sure you want go through with this? What with the murders and all, Waterford Point isn't exactly the world's number one vacation spot. You might be better off in Rockland or Searsport."

"I'll be fine," Rachel told her.

Maddie shrugged. "Suit yourself. Just be thankful I'm not putting you up down the hall." She pointed toward a closed door some distance from the stairs.

"Why?"

"Because that was Caroline's room."

"Caroline?"

Maddie nodded. "Came here from out of town, just like you. Little less than a month ago. Wasn't here two days when it happened."

"When what happened?"

"They found her in the woods out back," Maddie said. "She was Weeping Willow's first victim."

This was the second reference Maddie had made to Weeping Willow and Rachel once again stifled the urge to ask for details. She could see that Maddie was deeply affected by this death, her eyes filled with the kind of fear usually reserved for very late, very dark nights.

This woman Caroline's murder had obviously been the start of something horrible here in Waterford Point and the fact that the victim had been staying in this very house—had been found in the woods nearby—was a surprising coincidence.

It would also explain Sheriff Chavaree's sensitivity.

Had he been living here when Caroline was killed?

That would certainly raise some concerns—unfairly or not—about his ability to do his job, and she didn't doubt he had been struggling with those questions ever since.

But Rachel resisted the urge to dig deeper. Had to keep reminding herself that she was *not* here for a story.

Throw in Maddie's mention of a ghost, however, and she had to admit she saw a compelling mystery developing.

"I'll tell you," Maddie said. "I haven't been able to bring myself to go into that room. Haven't even made the bed. So consider yourself lucky, dear. Although, I suppose it's bad enough you'll even be *this* close. Thank goodness I'm staying downstairs."

Unlike Maddie, Rachel wasn't bothered that she'd be sleeping down the hall from the victim's room. She'd gone face-to-face with serial killers and sociopaths, so sharing the house with the specter of a dead girl didn't really concern her.

She could plainly see that Maddie was dying to keep talking about this, so she remained silent, doing her best not to prompt the woman.

This wasn't her affair.

Maddie seemed to get the message and five minutes later, Rachel was in her room with the door locked, her suitcase unpacked and a king-size bed waiting for her to crawl into it. Her flight and the trip across the bay had taken their toll, and all she wanted to do right now was nap.

Barring those last few minutes on the ferry, her

bouts with morning sickness had passed, but she found herself tiring more easily these days.

There was a time she wouldn't have dreamed of napping.

But things change, don't they?

Things always change.

RACHEL WAS ABOUT TO PUT her head on the pillow when her cell phone rang.

She sighed. What *now?*

Scooping the phone off the nightstand, she checked the screen but didn't recognize the number. She clicked it on and put it to her ear. "This had better be good."

"Rachel?" It was Janet Matlin, an assistant D.A. out of Los Angeles.

"Sorry, Janet, I'm a little out of sorts right now."

"Who wouldn't be, considering what you've been through. I just wanted to give you the heads-up."

"About what?"

"Lattimore made bail."

Rachel's chest tightened.

Emit Lattimore was a stone-cold, unrepentant sociopath, and the subject of Rachel's book in progress, *Ladykiller*—the book she had put on hold after Lattimore tried to strangle her during a contentious interview.

Lattimore's third wife went missing over six months ago, a disappearance that became a media sensation. The more the police looked into the disappearance, the more convinced they were that he was the likely perpetrator, especially since his two previous wives had died under suspicious circumstances.

One had taken a fall down some stairs, and the other had been shot by an intruder while Lattimore was reportedly away on a hunting trip. Lattimore had been a suspect in both deaths, but there had never been enough evidence for an arrest, let alone a trial and conviction.

And it didn't help that he was a former L.A. County medical examiner. Even Rachel's father had worked with him once or twice.

But Rachel was convinced his luck was running out and had begun writing the book in anticipation of that inevitability. She had pressed him hard during the interview, pushing a lot of buttons, but he'd been arrogant enough to think he could outmaneuver her. She caught him in a glaring contradiction and apparently his oversize ego couldn't take it. He suddenly snapped, leaping across the table, his face full of fury.

The memory was fresh in her mind, and she'd never forget those black, malevolent eyes boring into her, or those rough, oversize hands going for her throat. And knowing that he was out on bail after only a week behind bars didn't give her any comfort. Even if he was three thousand miles away.

"You still there, Rachel?"

She shook off the memory. "Can't you get a judge to consider revoking bail?"

"We're working on it but there aren't any guarantees. In the meantime, you might want to think about getting out of town for a bit."

"Already done," she said.

"Oh? Where are you?"

Rachel was about to respond, when Janet cut her off. "Wait, never mind. I don't want to know. Just stay there for a while."

That was certainly the plan.

The irony was that Rachel had booked this trip before Lattimore had become a threat. She had intended to use the time to finish writing *Ladykiller*, but that idea went out the window the moment he tried to wrap his hands around her throat. She couldn't be objective about him anymore, and objectivity was her stock in trade.

Rachel may have been tough-skinned, but she was also human. And Lattimore scared the heck out of her.

"You think he'd actually try to come after me?"

"He's a misogynist of the worst kind, Rachel, and

you wounded his ego. But if he doesn't know where you are…"

"Small comfort, believe me."

"Don't worry, we're doing our best to keep an eye on him and I'll be pushing to revoke. Even if we never find his wife, we at least have enough with the attempted assault to put him away for quite a while."

"Promises, promises," Rachel said quietly.

And promises were too often broken.

Chapter Three

Nick Chavaree couldn't remember a time he'd been so frustrated.

He didn't generally think of himself as an unhappy guy. He was usually pretty genial, as a matter of fact. But this last month in Waterford Point had been something of a nightmare. A nightmare he wouldn't wish on any cop in the known universe.

It was bad enough that he had three murder victims in as many weeks, all with their heads bashed in. But the fact that the first one had happened right under his nose, while he was *sleeping* for godsakes, had him wondering about his ability to serve his community.

It wasn't as if Nick was a stranger to violence. He'd spent five years in the Marines, running his own squad in the desert. But hunting down the Taliban in Afghanistan wasn't quite the same as gathering evidence at a local crime scene, and he wasn't afraid to admit that he was a little out of his depth here.

Throw Rachel Hudson into the mix and his bad month was about to get worse. He'd read all of her books—enjoyed them, as a matter of fact—but the thought that he might become the subject of one didn't sit well. And as beautiful as she might be, he didn't relish the idea of her sticking her cute little nose into this investigation.

Such as it was.

"You gonna eat that chicken or just stare at it all night along?"

Nick looked up from his plate at Charlie Tevis, who sat across the table from him. Charlie was one of his best deputies and they often had dinner together. They were sitting in a booth near the back of the Bayside Grill, the busiest and best of Waterford's handful of restaurants.

Charlie was a big guy with an equally genial attitude that hadn't been diminished by the recent turn of events.

"If you don't want it," he said, "slide that plate over here."

"How do you do it, Charlie?"

"Eat so much? I guess I was just born hungry."

"No," Nick said. "How do you stay so cheerful in the face of what's been going on around here?"

Charlie thought about it a moment, then leaned back. "It's all about attitude. I learned a long time ago that it's pointless to take life too seriously."

"You don't think three back-to-back murders in a town this size is serious?"

"Of course I do. Serious as a heart attack. But I don't see any point in moping about it. We'll catch this son of a gun sooner or later."

"That's what I keep telling myself."

"Don't you worry, he's bound to slip up. Assuming what we're talking about here is human."

Nick stared at him. "Don't tell me you're buying into this Weeping Willow nonsense."

Charlie shrugged. "If I were, I wouldn't be the only one. Putting this off on a ghost might explain a whole heckuva lot of—"

"Shut your trap, Tevis."

The voice came from behind Nick, but he didn't have to turn around to know who it was.

He braced himself for the assault.

A moment later, Bill Burgess slid in next to him and stared pointedly at Charlie. "We don't need that kind of talk coming from our own law enforcement officers."

Burgess was a former Rockland County judge and a smarmy, self-important jerk who had managed to get himself elected mayor—another mystery Nick had yet to solve.

"The day I start listening to you," Charlie told him, "is the day I turn in my gun and badge."

"That can certainly be arranged."

Burgess and Charlie had gone to high school together and Nick knew there was no love lost between them. Charlie had once told Nick that when he was thinking about returning to Waterford Point, after living across the country for nearly three decades, he may have reconsidered the move if he'd known that Burgess was the new mayor.

But Charlie had always had a soft spot for Maine, and Waterford Point in particular, so he figured he'd do his best to turn lemons into lemonade.

So far it wasn't working.

"Your threats don't scare me, Bill, so don't even bother."

Burgess's eyes narrowed. "You think I wouldn't do it?"

"I think you're all yap and no follow-through, just like you were in—"

"Stop," Nick said. "Both of you. This isn't getting us anywhere."

Burgess's face was turning red, but he calmed himself.

"Sorry, Nick, but the last thing we need right

now is your men perpetuating ridiculous rumors." He swept an arm out, gesturing to the room. "Look at this place. Best diner in town and it's practically empty. You start talking ghosts and that's what Waterford Point will become. A ghost town. And we can't afford that right now. We're already strapped enough as it is."

"People are scared, Bill."

"Of course they are. That's my point. You need to catch this guy, Nick. We can't afford for this to go on much longer."

"That's easier said than done. The crime scenes are always pristine. We've got no evidence."

"Then find some."

"How? I've got five deputies, and we're all stretched thin right now. We spend half our time chasing down false leads, people calling in at every little bump in the night. I'm a small-town sheriff, Bill. I don't have the manpower or the expertise to handle a case like this."

"So what are you suggesting?"

"I think we should invite the Maine State Police to help us out."

Burgess shook his head, his tone adamant. "No, no, no," he said. "We bring the staties in, we'll only invite more publicity. We're trying to *contain* this thing, not expand it."

"I'm not a miracle worker. What do you want me to do?"

"I don't know. You've got some Native American blood in you. Can't you do a smoke dance or something? Figure this thing out?"

Nick just stared at him.

Had he really just said that?

Charlie shook his head in disgust. "You are one amazing piece of work, Burgess."

Burgess glared at him, then got to his feet, shifting his gaze to Nick. "Look, Nick, I like you. The whole town likes you. But I'm starting to wonder if appointing you sheriff was a bad idea."

"You didn't appoint me," Nick said.

Burgess studied him a moment and Nick could clearly see the contempt in his eyes. Nick didn't often run into outright bigots these days, but he knew one when he saw one.

"That may be true," Burgess said. "But I can fire you just the same." He leaned in close. "And if you don't solve this case pronto, kemosabe, you'll be heading right back to the reservation."

Then he turned on his heels and walked away.

RACHEL COULDN'T SLEEP. After over an hour of tossing and turning and trying not to think about all the stuff that was plaguing her, she finally gave up and decided to find a place to go to dinner instead.

When she walked into the Bayside Grill, the last person she expected to find there was Sheriff Nick Chavaree.

He was sitting in a booth in back with one of his deputies, and as the hostess escorted her to a table, she could feel his gaze on her.

He probably thought she was stalking him.

She buried her face in the menu and was trying to decide between a chef's or Cobb salad, when Chavaree approached and sat down at her table.

He didn't look happy.

"You don't give up, do you?"

Rachel put the menu down and sighed. "I told you, Sheriff, I'm not interested in your case. Really. It's the furthest thing from my mind right now."

"Yet you just happen to show up here?"

Those eyes of his could melt stone.

"Maddie suggested it, okay? She says it's the best diner in town—and there aren't exactly a whole lot of choices."

"I wish I could believe you."

"You don't have to, but it's the truth. I've had my fill of murder and mayhem for a while. I'm just here to recharge the batteries."

She could see that he still wasn't buying it, but

what could she say to change his mind? He looked tired and overtaxed and she instinctively wanted to comfort him somehow.

She wasn't quite sure where that instinct was coming from but it was there. Something about this guy brought it out in her.

Something beyond his good looks.

"So why do I still get the feeling I'll wind up in your next book?" he said.

Rachel shook her head. "I'm already in the middle of another project. Besides, I'm putting the career on hold for the time being. Until I get some things sorted out." She sighed. "Look, I'd be lying to you if I didn't admit that this Weeping Willow angle is very compelling, but—"

He stiffened. "You know about that?"

"Your friend Maddie likes to talk a lot. But don't worry, I didn't push her for details. I don't really want to know any. In fact, the less I know, the better."

"Why is that?"

She was about to explain when Chavaree's deputy came over, pocketing a cell phone as he approached.

His voice was full of tension. "Nick, that was De-Mille. We need to go. Now."

Chavaree looked up at him with concern. "What's wrong?"

"We've got a situation." The deputy leaned toward Chavaree now and whispered in his ear.

Rachel couldn't hear what was being said, but she didn't need to.

One of the handy little skills she'd picked up over the years was the ability to read lips. She didn't always get it right but she came close at least half of the time, and even from this angle she knew exactly what was being said.

"They found another body."

Chapter Four

As Rachel watched them go out the door, she tried to remain seated. Tried to quell the excitement that rose in her chest as she'd watched the deputy's lips move.

She even went so far as to order a Cobb salad.

But as she sat there, thinking about those words, she felt a need coming on, the need she'd carried with her ever since she was thirteen and read her first true crime book.

They found another body.

Back then, when her friends were all reading *Teen Beat* and fawning over rock singers and sitcom stars, Rachel would devour monthly issues of *True Detective* and *Crime Scene*. She'd had to sneak them into her room and read them late at night because she knew her parents wouldn't approve.

And if her father had known that she'd peeked at his murder files more than once—the ones he kept in a locked desk drawer—he would've had a fit, even though he'd made it clear that he wanted her to follow in his footsteps one day.

They found another body.

Resist, Rachel, resist.

Don't prove yourself a liar.

Yet despite all her protests to Sheriff Chavaree, she *couldn't* resist. Before she could stop herself, she was on her feet, tossing money onto the table and headed outside to her rented car.

She heard a siren now, wailing in the gathering darkness, and she knew it was likely an ambulance on its way to the crime scene.

As she climbed in behind the wheel, she tried again to convince herself to let it go, to simply start the car and drive straight back to the Waterford Inn. But she knew even before she turned the key that would never happen.

And a minute later, as she sat near the main road with her engine idling, she saw a deputy's cruiser streak by.

Putting her transmission into gear, she fell in behind it and followed.

THE DEPUTY DROVE TOWARD the hills, quickly catching up to two other squad cars on a lonely stretch of road that wound through the forest.

Rachel tailed them a good distance behind. It was well past sunset now and the farther up the hill they went, the darker it got. The moon was high but it did little to illuminate the area, and that ever-present, living, breathing mist clung to the trees.

She saw mailboxes along the side of the road and thought this must be where some of the richer residents of Waterford Point lived. The place had a rustic but well-tended feel, and the trees and mist no doubt hid some very formidable New England homes.

The sheriff's cruisers came to a stop in the middle of the road. The ambulance was already there. In the wash of the cruiser's headlights Rachel saw a few deputies and emergency personnel attending the scene.

Pulling to the side, she killed her own headlights and sat watching through the windshield, knowing it wasn't too late to back out of this.

She thought about Chavaree and his reluctance to believe her. She guessed when it came down to it, she was proving him right. Her motive for coming to Waterford Point may have had nothing to do with his case, but here she was, already in working mode, and motivation didn't much matter at this point.

She felt a stab of guilt, thinking about those intense brown eyes looking at her from across the table, his gaze searching hers as he tried to decide whether he could trust her.

Apparently, he couldn't.

But if Rachel always gave in to her guilt, she wouldn't have four bestselling books in the stores, would she? Let alone a career. And while she had no real details and no idea if Chavaree's case was interesting enough to sustain five hundred manuscript pages, the potential was just too great to ignore.

She dug around in her purse until she found her miniature flashlight; she carried it wherever she went. It wasn't big but it would be bright enough to get her through the woods so she could take a closer look at the crime scene.

Glancing at the activity ahead, she climbed out of her car door. The beams of police Maglites criss-crossed in the trees.

After checking for cars Rachel crossed the road and stepped into the thick cluster of Eastern pine. She flicked on the light, keeping it low and aimed at the ground for fear one of the deputies might spot her.

The forest was nearly impenetrable here, thanks in large part to the mist. There were no pathways to guide her so she'd have to forge her own, doing her best to stay quiet in the process. If she went up and to the right, she should be able to circle around and place herself just above the crime scene.

Rachel had never been afraid of the dark, but the moment she started up the hill, the fallen tree branches crackling faintly beneath her shoes, the oddest feeling overcame her.

As if someone was watching her.

She looked back at the road but it was empty except for her car. She had parked near a mailbox, next to a tree-sheltered driveway. She knew there was a house back there somewhere but she doubted anyone inside would be able to see her.

Yet the sensation didn't go away.

Had her run-in with Emit Lattimore turned her into a paranoid wimp?

Ignoring the feeling, she continued her climb up the hillside.

The ground was loose and damp, and had trouble keeping her footing. She banged her knee against a piece of fallen timber and almost poked her eye out on a low-hanging branch. She somehow managed to do it all quietly and with her dignity still intact, and she soon found herself crouching in a cluster of pines about a hundred yards above the deputies' flashlight beams.

They stood in a small clearing just off the road, those beams pointed at a body that lay at their feet on a bed of pine needles.

A man's body.

Chavaree stood over him, and Rachel sensed a change in the sheriff's body language. The quiet anger he'd displayed in the restaurant and in Maddie's foyer seemed to have abandoned him now. He seemed vulnerable somehow, as if he was taking this death hard. Not as just another homicide, but as a personal assault.

And again, she had to admit that he was right. He'd told her he had a feeling he'd wind up in one of her books, and what she saw here was the hero at the center of the storm.

He certainly fulfilled the requirements. The dark good looks. The outer strength. He was the kind of guy who commanded your attention the moment he walked into a room, yet beneath that cool self-assurance was a huge capacity for empathy and understanding.

Just what Rachel needed in her life.

With sudden alarm she realized that she wasn't looking at Chavaree as the center of *a* story, but of *her* story, and she had no idea where such a notion had come from. It had snuck up on her without warning.

Get a grip, girl. This isn't about you.

As she watched, Chavaree got down on his haunches and scooped up a handful of pine needles and dirt, closing his eyes as he let it sift through his fingers.

What was he up to?

A prayer of some kind?

Then he opened his eyes, stared at the body for a moment and got to his feet, turning to say something to one of his deputies—the one she'd seen with him in the diner.

She was too far away to read his lips, but she knew everything she needed to know by the look on his face.

The dead man was a friend of Chavaree's.

"I THINK I WENT TO HIGH school with this guy," Charlie said. "Maybe that's the connection we've been looking for. The victims all went to high school together."

Nick stared at the body. He hadn't known Russ Webber all that well, but they'd gone fishing a few times, shared a couple beers and he'd liked the guy even if he *had* been a bit guarded. Webber was a local real estate agent who had helped Nick secure a contractor for the renovations on his house.

Waterford Point was a small town, but it wasn't that small—it boasted a population of seven thousand. The other three victims had been virtual strangers to Nick, including Caroline.

So this death was a little more personal to him.

Seeing Russ lying there with his head bashed in was like a kick to the gut. It reminded him of his days in Afghanistan, whenever one of the men from his unit went down. He was their commanding officer so he didn't know them as well as the boys in the trenches did, but it hurt just the same.

Charlie's observation about high school connections was a good one, but it was one Nick had already considered. The victims were all around the same age—mid-forties—and had all attended Jefferson High during the same four-year period. Even Caroline had spent a couple of semesters there before moving away.

He remembered when she took the room at Maddie's. She'd seemed a little skittish as she introduced herself. She was an attorney, she'd told him, who had come to Waterford Point to meet with a potential client. She'd never mentioned who that client was, and Nick had never been able to find out.

It could well have been her killer.

Of course, that was over three weeks ago, before Nick or anyone else had been looking for a pattern. And while the high school angle was a good start, it simply wasn't enough to hang an investigation on.

"That might be helpful," he told Charlie, "if there was more than one high school around here. But if that's the connection, then we've got a couple thousand potential victims out there."

"Including me," Charlie said. "Maybe I should sleep with my gun under my pillow."

"Might not be a bad idea." Nick scanned the area. "Where's the witness? The kid who found the body?"

"Over here," someone said, and Nick found Joe DeMille standing near a tree with a teenager in a sweatshirt and jogging shorts.

The kid's eyes were blank. He looked shell-shocked.

Nick and Charlie went over to him, and Nick said, "What's your name, son?"

"Kenny Gray." His voice trembled slightly.

"You live around here?"

The kid nodded. "Just down the road. I'm training for cross-country and was out for a run when I found him. It's lucky I saw him at all."

"Why's that?"

"There wasn't much light by then and this clearing is pretty well hidden from the road. I usually pass right by it."

"So what made you stop this time?"

The kid hesitated and Nick could see that he was scared. "Take it easy, Kenny. You're safe with us. Just tell us what happened."

"It was the girl," he said.

"Girl?"

"I heard her. Here in the trees. At first I thought she might be hurt or something, so I came to see if I could help."

Nick's gut tightened. He knew exactly where this was headed but hoped he was wrong. "What did you hear?"

"She was crying. Just like in the stories."

Nick and Charlie exchanged glances.

"What stories?" Charlie asked.

"Come on, man, you know what stories. The ones about Weeping Willow. The ghost who walks the woods."

Nick sighed. "You sure it wasn't a bird of some kind?"

The kid shook his head. "I heard her as plain as day. Crying like a lost little girl."

Nick and Charlie exchanged another glance. This wasn't the first time a witness had told them this. Even Maddie had claimed she'd heard the crying the night of Caroline's death.

But Nick wasn't buying it. This was just a form of mass hysteria. People latching on to a thirty-year-old folktale and convincing themselves it was true. Either that or the killer was playing some kind of game.

"You sure you didn't hear this *after* you found the

body? You must've been pretty shook up. Could've been imagining—"

"I swear to God it was her, Sheriff. I wouldn't have come in here if I hadn't heard her."

Nick nodded. He knew he could keep pushing the kid, but that would only back him into a corner and Nick doubted he'd change his story. Maddie hadn't changed hers.

Of course, there were people in the world who were convinced they'd seen UFOs or had been abducted by aliens, and that was even less believable than a ghost who walked the woods.

But who was Nick to judge? His own culture was full of stories that most of the world didn't buy into, and when it came down to it, people believed what they wanted to believe.

His job was to figure out how those beliefs impacted his investigation, and in this case he didn't think it mattered all that much. Ghost stories were great around a campfire, but despite what the witnesses had said, he had no doubt that the killer they were after was all too human.

Nick just wished the guy was a little *more* human and would make a mistake.

He nodded to the kid. "Thank you, Kenny. We'll need you to come into the office tomorrow, make a formal statement."

"What about school?"

"I think you can afford to miss a couple—"

A sound cut Nick off. The snap of a branch up on the hillside and a soft but unmistakable yelp.

Five flashlight beams shot toward the trees and one of Nick's deputies shouted, "There's someone up there!"

Then they all started up the hill.

RACHEL RAN.

Couldn't believe how stupid she was.

She'd been trying to get a closer look at the activity below, slowly working her way from tree to tree, wanting to hear what was being said, when she foolishly forgot to look where she was going and tripped over a fallen branch.

Idiot.

Now she was practically flying through the trees, going back the way she came, her flashlight doing very little to guide her as panic rose in her throat. Branches thrashed behind her, footsteps and shouts in her wake, as she tried to remember every turn she'd made on the way here.

But that was impossible, of course, not to mention ridiculous, and the deputies behind her were stronger and faster than she was. Even if she managed to avoid falling on her butt and get to her car, they'd be on top of her before she even had the door open.

So she did the only sensible thing she could.

She stopped in her tracks.

Turned around.

Put her hands up.

"Don't shoot," she shouted. "It's only me."

Then the trees directly in front of her rustled and Nick Chavaree burst through, shining his flashlight beam directly in her face.

"Freeze!"

Then he paused, his voice now full of scorn and disbelief as he realized who he was looking at. "You have *got* to be kidding me."

Chapter Five

This wasn't the first time Rachel had been in the back seat of a sheriff's cruiser. Such things were a hazard of the profession—like getting pine needles stuck in your teeth.

And your hair. And on your clothes.

She was a walking, breathing *Pinus strobus*.

She said, "It's your own fault, you know."

They had been driving for several minutes now and Chavaree glanced at her in his rearview mirror. "Come again?"

"If you hadn't sat down at my table tonight, I'd be in my room right now, doing a crossword puzzle and minding my own business."

"Somehow you don't strike me as the crossword puzzle type," he said.

True. Rachel didn't have the patience for crosswords. She was more of a Daily Jumble girl. "I know you think I was lying."

"Think?"

"Every word out of my mouth was the truth. But I'm a creature of impulse. When I heard what your deputy said about finding another body, I didn't think, I just reacted."

"Poorly," he said. "You're what my grandmother calls a *mdupina.*"

"A what?"

"*Mdupina.* A headache."

Rachel bristled slightly. Emit Lattimore had told her she was "giving him a migraine" shortly before he leaped across the table at her. But that wasn't something she wanted to think about at the moment.

"So what now? You toss me in a jail cell and throw away the key?"

"Believe me, I'm tempted."

"But?"

"But when it comes down to it," he said, "you didn't really do all that much harm and I'm inclined to forgive and forget. With strings attached, of course."

Rachel didn't like the sound of that. "What kind of strings?"

"You agree to leave Waterford Point. Go back home and finish that project you claim you're in the middle of. Assuming that wasn't a lie, too."

"I told you, everything I said—"

"I know, I know, but I think you can understand why I might be a little skeptical."

Rachel did, but wasn't about to say it out loud. That would only bolster his argument, and part of her wanted him to know that she really *could* be trusted.

She wasn't sure why this mattered to her so much. Maybe it had something to do with that moment of vulnerability she'd seen in him at the crime scene. She wanted to appeal to that softer, empathetic side— which was a tall order now that she'd been branded a liar.

And a headache.

"*Mdupina,* huh?"

"That's right," he said.

"Well, maybe I'm the kind of *mdupina* you need right now."

"Meaning what?"

"I think you could use my help on this case."

This got another glance in the mirror. "You do, do you?"

"You've read my books. You know how thorough I am. And you know that I know my way around a murder investigation. In fact, I can pretty much guarantee I've been around more crime scenes than you've ever dreamed of."

"I lost a friend tonight, so *dream* isn't a word I'd use right now."

"I also spent five years on the police beat for the *Los Angeles Tribune,* I've got a master's degree in criminology and my father was one of the LAPD's top homicide investigators."

"What is this, a sales pitch?"

"Something like that."

"So why didn't you become a cop?"

"Because I'm impatient. And I don't like rules."

He smothered a laugh. "That much is obvious."

"So what do you have to lose?" she said. "We can sit down, you tell me what evidence you have so far, I'll tell you what I think and everyone'll be happy."

Chavaree pulled to a stop in front of the inn and turned to look at her. "You really don't have a very high opinion of me, do you?"

Rachel was surprised. "Why would you say that?"

"I don't know, maybe it's your condescending tone? Like I'm some hick cop who's in over his head and doesn't know how to swim, let alone tread water? I get enough of that from the mayor."

"I don't think that at all. I just want to—"

"I know what you want, Ms. Hudson. And I remember what you wrote in your last book about that sheriff in Waco. You eviscerated the guy."

"That was different."

"How?"

"Because *he* deserved it," she said. "He was arrogant and self-righteous and too full of himself to realize he had no clue what he was doing."

"Says you. Maybe he was just annoyed by the fact that you were dipping your toes in his pond—a feeling I can appreciate."

Chavaree put the car in park, then climbed out and came around to open her door. "What do you say we stick to my original plan? You get out of town, I don't put you in jail."

Ouch.

He gestured and she climbed out. "You're making a mistake, Sheriff."

"Apparently I make a lot of mistakes." He closed her door, moved back around to his side. "Your rental car will be waiting for you here when you wake up in the morning. I'd suggest you use it."

Then he climbed back in and drove away.

"What happened, dear? You look like somebody knocked the snot out of you on the playground."

Rachel felt like it, too. Not only was she still covered in pine needles and a good amount of dirt, she felt humiliated. Not so much by Chavaree's rejection, but because everything he'd said about her had been right.

She *had* come across like a condescending jerk. And that was the last thing she'd wanted to do.

Convinced this whole Lattimore-slash-pregnancy distraction was throwing her off her game, she said, "I'm pretty sure I deserved it."

Maddie smiled. She was seated behind the check-in counter with a calculator and a pile of receipts in front of her. "That was Nick's car out there. You two have your first little spat?"

Rachel balked. "Our what?"

"I saw the way you gawked at him when he came down those stairs, dearie. He's a fine-looking man."

"That may be true, but I don't even know the guy."

Maddie's smile broadened. "But you'd like to, wouldn't you? And I don't think *he'd* mind all that much, either."

Rachel had already thought Maddie was a little wacky. Now she was convinced the woman was completely off her rocker.

"Is that why he's told me to leave town twice in one day?"

Maddie waved a hand, dismissing the thought. "Oh, that'll pass. Once he gets done being a man and gettin' all pushed out of shape over nothing, he'll be apologizing and asking you to stay."

"I highly doubt it," Rachel said.

"Doubt it all you want, but he's been renting a room here for close to four months now. You learn a lot about someone when they're living under the same roof."

"Well, I hate to break it to you, Maddie, but you don't know him quite as well as you think you do."

"Uh-huh," she said. "We'll see."

She abruptly went back to her calculator and receipts and seemed to have forgotten that Rachel was even there. Rachel waited a moment, then shook her head in exasperation and trudged up the stairs.

She might as well shower and pack.

Contrary to what Maddie might think, Nick Chavaree was not about to change his mind and Rachel didn't see any point in putting up a fuss. There were other places she could go to get away. If Chavaree didn't want her here, then so be it.

Closing herself in her room, she grabbed her laptop, plopped herself on her bed, then revved up the internet browser and clicked on her favorite travel website.

Maybe she should go overseas for a while. Check out Paris or St. Tropez. Run topless on the beach before she really started showing.

Better than running through a forest with a bunch of sheriff's deputies after you, wasn't it?

Yet as she clicked through the travel site's menus, her mind wouldn't stay focused on what she was looking at. Instead she kept thinking about that body in the clearing and Nick Chavaree standing over it, defeated.

She still knew next to nothing about his case but she saw how it was affecting him, and that made her even more curious about it.

Clicking a search page, she typed in the words "weeping willow" and "Waterford Point," but all she got were a few botany websites, a social network page for a British pop singer and a link for an apartment complex in Florida. She continued clicking through the results until she finally found something of interest on the third screen, buried in a university website.

It was an article that was several years old titled "Mythology in Modern Society". Rachel clicked the link and discovered a student paper written nearly a decade ago about the persistence of myth in our lives, despite our modern sophistication.

It was a poorly written piece, but the thinking that went into it was sound. Toward the end of the article the writer gave an example of contemporary mythology, pointing to a story that had grown out of a tragedy in Waterford Point, Maine.

Bingo.

Thirty years ago, a shy young Native American girl was adopted by a Waterford Point couple after her parents were killed in an automobile accident. The girl, who had been born and partly raised on a nearby reservation called Indian Island, was shy and reclusive and had trouble fitting in with the kids at the local high school.

Nobody knew for sure what happened, but eight months after the girl moved to town, her house burnt to the ground, taking her and her adoptive parents along with it.

That would have been that, except the medical examiner discovered signs of blunt force trauma on the bodies and investigators suspected murder and arson. But at the time the article was written, no one had been arrested.

Waterford Point residents claimed they often heard the dead girl crying in the night, and as the story grew over the years, it was said that she was out there waiting to take revenge against her family's killer.

Out of the tragedy, a modern myth was born. The myth of the Weeping Willow. The ghost who walked the woods.

Rachel lay there a moment, staring at the screen.

She didn't scare easily, but her gaze immediately shifted to the view outside her window.

To the woods.

There were four people dead now, and the first one—Caroline—had been found right out there.

Not two hundred yards away.

She won't rest until we're all dead, Maddie had told her.

Rachel stared at the mist-shrouded trees and shuddered. She didn't believe in ghosts but that didn't keep the fear from skittering up her spine. She felt goose bumps tickle her scalp and immediately closed the computer, deciding she'd read more than enough for one night.

She thought about that poor girl and what she must have gone through.

A girl the town had shunned and was now afraid of.

Rachel remembered the feeling she'd had as she crossed from her car tonight, moving into the trees.

The feeling that she was being watched.

She knew the notion was ridiculous but she couldn't shake it off.

Was the girl really out there?

And if she was, who was next on her list?

Chapter Six

Rachel was awakened by a phone call.

Groaning, she fumbled for her cell on the nightstand and checked the time.

Seven in the morning.

How the heck had that happened? One minute she was obsessing over Weeping Willow, the next she was in lullaby land.

She hadn't even bathed, for godsakes. She was still wearing her clothes from last night and the bed was now full of dirt and pine needles.

Ugh.

Maddie would probably have her head.

Stabbing the Call button, she put the phone to her ear and muttered something only slightly intelligible into the receiver.

"Rachel? It's Janet again. Did I wake you?"

Rachel blinked a few times, tried to clear her mind. "What time is it there?"

"Four o'clock. I've been up all night."

"Why? What's going on?"

"I managed to get the judge to revoke Lattimore's bail."

Rachel was suddenly awake now. She sat up, overjoyed. "Really? How did you—"

"Don't get too excited. That's only the good part. I'm afraid I have some bad news, too."

Rachel's heart started thumping. She tried to calm herself. "What happened?"

"Lattimore's disappeared."

Rachel listened quietly as Janet went on to explain that they'd had a man watching him, but Lattimore had outsmarted the guy and given them the slip. They'd been sitting on his house ever since, but they'd seen no sign of him and were concerned he may have left town.

"We found his car. It was parked at an expired meter at the airport, short-term parking."

"Wonderful. Do you have any idea where he went?"

"We're checking with the airlines, but there's no way to tell at this point." She paused. "It gets worse, I'm afraid."

"How?"

"We found several of your books in his car, along with some newspaper articles about you. Interviews, that sort of thing. I don't want to alarm you, but one of the photos of you was mutilated. He cut out your mouth and eyes."

Sudden dread bubbled in the pit of Rachel's stomach. "Do you think he knows where I am?"

"*I* don't even know, remember? And I don't see how he could. But you might want to keep your eyes open. Maybe contact the local police."

Rachel almost laughed. Been there, done that. "When did all this happen?"

"Last night, right after I spoke to you. The only reason the judge revoked bail was because Lattimore fled town."

"Half a day late and two dollars short," Rachel muttered. Something her father always said when a case got the better of him.

The problem with Lattimore was that he had money. A lot of it. He had been born into a rich family and spent his life drifting from one disaster to the next—drugs, booze, parties, women—before finally he pulled himself together, got a medical degree and found work in law enforcement.

But the more Rachel dug into his life, the more repugnant she'd found him. His mother had been alcoholic and neglectful, and Lattimore had developed a decided mistrust and hatred for women. Rachel was convinced that the detour into police work had more to do with providing him cover than actually serving the public.

Lattimore was a bad penny, and the idea that he was out there somewhere chilled her to the bone.

"You okay, kiddo?"

"I've been better," she said.

"Don't worry, we'll find him. If you want to come home, we can put you under protection."

Rachel thought about this, but didn't relish the idea of going back to California.

Better to take her chances here.

Or in St. Tropez.

The whole idea behind coming to Waterford Point had been to cut herself off from the world. So she hadn't told anyone where she was going. Not her friends. Her editor. Or even her parents.

So unless Lattimore was some kind of clairvoyant, it seemed unlikely that he would be able to find her. Chances were pretty good that he was already on his way to St. Tropez himself, too busy avoiding capture to bother with the likes of her.

It was probably best that she stay put.

Of course, convincing Nick Chavaree not to toss her into a jail cell was another story altogether.

"Rachel? I've already spoken to our witness protection people, so if you want it, it's yours."

She relaxed a little. Everything would be fine.

Wouldn't it?

"No," she said. "I'll stay where I am. Just catch the guy, okay?"

"Believe me, it's our first priority."

Rachel thanked her and clicked off, desperately hoping that she wasn't Lattimore's first priority.

SHE WAS STILL THINKING about it when she surprised Nick Chavaree in the bathroom.

Clad in her favorite terry cloth robe, she was hoping to finally step into the shower and wash last night's debacle off her, when she pushed the door open and found Chavaree standing shirtless at the sink, scraping a razor along his throat.

He flinched at the sight of her. Drew blood. Rachel saw it before he did and scrambled for some toilet paper.

"Oh, my God," she said. "You're hurt. I'm so sorry."

Wadding up the tissue, she moved to blot his neck. To her surprise, he let her.

"I am such an idiot," she said. "I should've knocked before barging in here."

"It's okay. I think I'll live."

He seemed to be in a better mood this morning. Softer. Less hostile toward her. In fact, he didn't seem hostile at all. Maybe this was a good time to talk to him about staying.

As she dabbed at the wound, it suddenly occurred to her that he was half-naked. His skin was smooth and deeply muscled, marred only by a few scars near his chest.

Knife scars, from the looks of them.

There was something in his manner that suggested the military to her, something about the way he held himself, and she wondered if he'd gotten the scars in combat.

As he took the tissue from her and continued blotting away the blood, Rachel stepped back and couldn't help admiring the cut of his body. She had to force herself not to openly gape at the guy.

"I really am sorry," she said.

He shrugged. "Accidents happen."

"Maybe, but it seems like I'm just one big walking disaster zone these days."

She was hoping to turn this into a conversation about sticking around.

He looked at her now, briefly catching her gaze before his eyes widened slightly and shifted focus.

Then he smiled. "I guess that's probably true."

He quickly looked away and it took Rachel a moment to realize that he'd been focused on her chest. Glancing down, she discovered to her horror that the top of her robe had fallen open and she was showing quite a bit more than cleavage.

Her right breast was exposed.

Mortified, she quickly adjusted the robe and backed out of the doorway, not wanting him to see her blush.

He'd already seen enough.

"I'll…I'll talk to you at breakfast," she muttered.

"Wait," he said with a chuckle in his voice. "You don't have to run away on my account."

Oh, my God, Rachel thought.

Oh, my God.

NICK WAS STILL MUSING over the encounter in the bathroom when Maddie put a plate of bacon and eggs in front of him. He wasn't normally a lecherous guy, but he was male, and he had to admit that this morning's little peep show had been a pleasant diversion.

More than pleasant.

Rachel was a stunning woman.

The truth was, he'd been thinking about her ever since he'd dropped her off last night. He felt terrible for treating her so badly.

Yes, he'd been annoyed, and no, she shouldn't have been sneaking around the crime scene, but he knew his annoyance had more to do with his own failures, not hers.

Rachel's only real crime was being in the wrong place at the wrong time and having the misfortune to trigger the anger and frustration that had been simmering inside him for days.

Whether or not she had lied to him about her reasons for coming to Waterford Point didn't really matter much now. And while her offer of help may have been a teensy bit self-serving—she was, after all, looking for a story to write—he was convinced it had also been genuine.

And in the light of day, the idea didn't strike him as entirely ridiculous.

Judging by her books, Rachel Hudson had a keen mind, a good eye for detail and a lot of practical experience in the field. And with Bill Burgess refusing to let him bring in the state police, Nick figured he needed all the assistance he could get.

But none of this had much to do with why he couldn't stop thinking about her. This wasn't about last night and his incivility, or her offer to help, or even the mishap in the bathroom this morning—not that he was complaining, mind you.

The *real* reason he couldn't stop thinking about her was the sheer force of her personality. She was bold and impetuous, yet at the same time surprisingly modest and self-effacing. And he had never in his life met a woman so…intriguing.

She was, he thought, one of a kind.

Of course, he'd already known that. Knew it the first time he read one of her books.

So maybe he was simply starstruck.

Maddie poured him a glass of orange juice and Nick tried to stop her. "Come on, Mad, you don't have to wait on me. Sit down and eat."

"As long as you're paying room and board, hot shot, I'll be serving breakfast and pouring the orange juice."

"What am I, a Roman king? Sit down."

"I'll sit when I'm good and ready. I've still got another guest to feed." She looked toward the stairs. "Although rumor has it you kicked her out last night."

Nick looked at her, feeling a little sheepish. "You heard about that, huh?"

"You should be proud of yourself, Nick. Treating her like that in her condition."

"Condition?"

"You really are dumb as rocks, aren't you? She's four months pregnant."

Nick paused, a bit taken aback. "How do you know that?"

"Don't forget what I used to do for a living. Besides, she told me."

Nick felt a stab of disappointment. Not because Rachel was pregnant. He hoped to have kids of his own, one day. But because the revelation meant that she most likely had a man in her life—which shouldn't have been a surprise, considering how lovely she was.

But then it wasn't as if Nick was planning to make a move or anything. They were from completely different coasts, and he doubted she had much interest in an insensitive hick like him. Especially after he'd just stared at her like a sex-deprived teenager.

Way to play it, Nick.

You're a heckuva guy.

Yet he felt disappointed nevertheless, and had to wonder why he was letting himself get so wrapped up in this woman.

Better to keep things professional and concentrate on the case.

He was just digging into his food when she came down the stairs, looking fresh from a shower, wearing a wool sweater and a pair of jeans.

"Sorry I'm late," she said to Maddie and took a seat across the table from Nick. She didn't look away or seem embarrassed at all. But she wasn't overly friendly, either.

Who could blame her?

Maddie headed toward the kitchen. "You're fine, dear. We just started a little early is all."

When she was gone, Nick and Rachel sat quietly listening to her clang around in the kitchen as Nick stared at his breakfast.

"I started packing," Rachel said. "I should be out of your hair before noon."

Nick put his fork down.

"Look," he said. "I want to apologize for last night. I overreacted."

She shook her head. "I had no business being at that crime scene."

"Let's forget about that, okay? I have a proposition for you."

Her eyebrows went up. "Proposition?"

"I want to take you up on your offer to help. I figure you can ride along with me, observe and comment, put me on the right track when you think I've been derailed. All I ask is that you don't write about it until the case has been put to bed."

"You aren't afraid I'll eviscerate you?"

He shrugged. "I have a feeling you'll be fair."

She furrowed her brow. "This is a sudden about-face. What changed your…" She paused. "You know that what happened in the bathroom was an accident, don't you?"

"Oh, I know. I saw the look on your face."

"I just don't want you to think I was trying to seduce you or something. That's not who I am."

"Don't worry, I believe you. No harm, no foul."

"So then what changed your mind about me helping you?"

He shrugged again. "Common sense."

"I thought you said I was a headache? What was the word you used?"

"Mdupina."

"What language is that?"

"Abenaki-Penobscot. But you don't hear it much anymore. My grandmother was full blood and she barely spoke it."

"That's a shame," Rachel said. "But whatever the case, I wouldn't want to have you reaching for the aspirin every ten minutes."

He grinned. "I'm willing to take my chances."

She was quiet a moment as she thought about it, but he could see a trace of relief on her face.

He had a feeling she'd been hoping all along that he'd change his mind and he sensed that something was troubling her.

Something unrelated to the case.

He didn't ask her what it was.

"Seriously," he said. "I really could use a fresh pair of eyes."

"All right," she told him. "It's a deal. But I think your eyes are just fine."

"What do you mean?"

"You pretty much proved that upstairs."

Chapter Seven

Rachel was relieved.

She had been planning to ask that Chavaree reconsider his edict, with a sincere promise that she'd keep her nose out of his business. His peace offering had come as a surprise and was more than she could have hoped for.

Now she was sitting in his cruiser again—the front seat this time—with the case file in her lap. They were headed to the home of Angela Webber, the latest victim's wife.

Chavaree had done the death notification late last night, but he told Rachel that he'd wanted to give Angela some breathing room before he formally questioned her. Give her a chance to grieve.

"That may have been a mistake, Sheriff. Unless you've completely ruled her out as a suspect."

"Call me Nick," he said. "Everyone does."

"Okay, Nick. But the comment still stands."

He nodded. "I think it's safe to assume Angela isn't the perpetrator."

"Why?"

"She isn't physically capable of it for one thing. She's an invalid. Has been for years."

"There's always murder for hire."

He considered this, then shook his head. "I don't buy it. I don't know her all that well, but whenever I saw her and Russ together I always got the feeling they were very much in love. That's something you can't fake."

Rachel thought about her relationship with Dan and had to agree. "You speaking from experience?"

"I'm afraid I'm what you'd call a few and far between guy."

"Oh? Afraid to commit?"

"Not at all," he said. "I just haven't found the right person yet. Call me selfish, but I want what Russ and Angela had. What my mother and father still have."

"You think you'll ever find it?"

She had doubts that she ever would. Especially after the Dan disaster and her pregnancy. There weren't too many men in the world who wanted to take on an entire family in one fell swoop, and finding the *right* one wouldn't be easy.

Nick smiled. "Despite appearances, I'm something

of an optimist. And you never know who's waiting around the next corner."

Their gazes briefly locked and Rachel felt a faint fluttering in her chest. She thought about him standing at that bathroom sink with his shirt off but quickly dismissed the image from her mind. That was her hormones talking, not her heart.

Nick was silent after that and she pushed away any thoughts of love or passion. She was here to work now, not play.

Opening the case file in her lap, she began reading the summaries of the three previous murders.

The first victim, Caroline Keller, was an attorney who lived and worked in Washington, D.C. She had come to Waterford Point, her secretary claimed, after receiving a phone call from a potential client who wanted to hire her for some contract work. But when the D.C. police went over the phone records, they found nothing coming from Maine. Caroline's current list of clients was meager and offered them no clues.

The second victim was a local bank teller named Ed Penski. His mother, with whom he had lived, said that he'd been very popular back in high school but became withdrawn and depressed after graduation and kept mostly to himself. She couldn't think of anyone who would want to kill him because he had no real friends and never spoke of any enemies.

The third victim was a divorced alcoholic named Sheila Malone who spent most of her time perched on a stool at the Scratching Post, a locals-only bar. Sheila had never been very discriminating when it came to bed partners, and there was some speculation that one of her many boyfriends had killed her. Most of the bar's regulars had alibis, however, and the two who didn't had both passed polygraph tests.

The only thing the victims had in common was that they were all approximately the same age, had all attended the same high school and had all been killed by blunt force trauma to the head. And in every case, the medical examiner believed a rock had been used.

Rachel immediately thought of the article she'd read last night. The Native American girl and her foster parents had reportedly died of blunt force trauma as well.

A coincidence?

Rachel didn't think so. Especially when you added in a fourth connection between the victims.

"What do you make of *this?*" she asked Nick.

He glanced at her. "What?"

She gestured to the file. "It says here that in each

case, either a witness or the victims themselves heard a girl crying outside their window."

"That's the claim," Nick said.

"You don't believe it?"

"I tend to take statements like that with a grain of salt."

"Why?"

He looked at her again. "Are you serious?"

"When three different witnesses say they heard the same thing, I tend to listen."

Nick returned his eyes to the road. "The Weeping Willow myth has been around for a few decades, but nobody with half a brain takes much stock in it."

"Yet they all claim they heard her."

"You know how it goes," he said. "The rumors started after the second murder and once it got circulated, people were making all kinds of wild claims. There's an old woman on Cedar who says Weeping Willow has been living in her basement for ten years."

"That still doesn't explain these witness statements."

"Think about it. This whole ghost idea is both scary and romantic at the same time. People hear something normal outside the window, like a bird crying or their neighbor's television, and turn it into something supernatural because it gives them a charge."

"You're saying they *want* it to be a ghost."

Nick nodded. "It's a lot more exciting that way, isn't it? And it gives you a nice little story to tell around the watercooler."

"But even Maddie said she heard the girl. The night Caroline died."

"I rest my case."

ANGELA WEBBER WAS A FRAIL, nearly translucent-skinned woman who wasn't more than a few years older than Rachel. She sat in a wheelchair in the living room of her home, her eyes red and swollen, a box of tissues on the table next to her.

The curtains were drawn and the room was dim and slightly claustrophobic. There were dolls every-where. On the sofa. On the mantel above the fire-place. Locked inside glass cases.

They were collector's dolls, the kind with porce-lain skin and vacant eyes.

Kind of like Angela Webber herself.

"I can't believe he's gone," she said. "Russell was everything to me."

They were seated across from her on the sofa, Rachel feeling as if the yellow-haired doll perched on the cushion next to her was watching her, carefully. Waiting for her to make a wrong move.

"I can only imagine how you feel," Nick said to Angela. "Russ was a great guy."

"He was, wasn't he? He made so much progress over the years."

"Progress?" Rachel asked.

Angela nodded. "Russ had a troubled childhood. He went through several bouts of depression in his youth."

"I didn't know that," Nick said. "You'd never tell by talking to him."

"Yes, well, thanks to his medication he managed to beat it most of the time. Plus he had me to contend with. Taking care of me was enough to distract him from the demons that plagued him."

"What sort of demons?"

"I'm not sure," she said. "There were some things Russ didn't share with me. Stories from his childhood. And I had sense enough not to press. We all have our secrets, don't we?"

Every single one of us, Rachel thought.

Nick said, "Can you think of anyone who want to hurt him? Any enemies he may have had?"

"I've been wondering about that ever since you told me last night. But people around here loved Russ. He was the kind of man who would go out of his way to help you. I can't even imagine why anyone would want him…" She faltered, grabbing for a tissue. "Why anyone would want him dead."

Tears started rolling down her cheeks and she dabbed them away. Rachel had been fortunate enough in her life to never lose anyone she loved, but she imagined the pain must be excruciating.

"What about the other victims?" she asked. "Did Mr. Webber know any of them?"

"Not that he mentioned. Waterford Point isn't as small a town as you might think it is, and we didn't run in the same social circles."

Nick said, "Do you have any idea why he was up on Blanchard Drive?"

"He has a couple of listings up there, I think. I assume he went to meet with a potential buyer."

"Do you know who this buyer might be?"

She shook her head. "There was a time I used to handle Russ's schedule, but those days are long gone." She paused a moment as another thought occurred to her. "But one thing I can tell you is that something was bothering him these last few days."

"Any idea what?" Nick asked.

"I can't be sure, but he'd been agitated lately. More than I've ever seen him."

"And you don't know why?"

Angela seemed to be gone for a moment, assaulted

by a memory. Then she said, "I just wish I'd paid more attention to him. Taken him more seriously."

Then her eyes welled up again and she dabbed at them with a trembling hand. Rachel thought about the article she'd read and decided to change the subject slightly.

"Mrs. Webber, your husband went to Jefferson High, correct?"

Angela nodded. "Yes, of course. Why?"

"I read a story last night about a young Native American girl who was killed here around the time your husband was in high school. I'm wondering if he ever mentioned it to you."

"You're talking about Weeping Willow, of course. Everyone here knows that story. Even transplants like me."

"I sometimes wish I didn't," Nick said, and Rachel had to wonder if this was his way of telling her to back off.

But she pressed on. "I only ask because she may have been a classmate of Mr. Webber's. And I'm curious to know if he ever mentioned the incident."

"Russ didn't talk much about that time in his life. He liked to concentrate on the positive."

"So you don't know whether he knew her?"

She closed her eyes a moment as she gathered herself. "I do know he was afraid of her."

Nick frowned. "What do you mean?"

"I honestly think that's why he was so agitated."

"Because of Weeping Willow?"

She nodded. "You see, I've never been much of a believer in fairy tales. You have the kind of health problems I have, you tend to look at the world with a very practical eye. Fairy tales only distract you from what needs to be done."

"And Russ?"

She smiled. Wistful. Melancholy. "He was a different animal altogether. He came to me the other night, white as a sheet, and said he thought we needed to get away from here for a while."

"Why?" Nick asked.

"Because he'd heard someone crying outside his window that night. And he was convinced it was Weeping Willow."

Rachel and Nick exchanged a look.

"Did you hear it, too?"

Angela shook her head. "We sleep in separate rooms these days. My nights are often restless and I didn't want to disturb him, poor dear."

"Do you mind if we take a look at his room?" Nick asked. "Just to be thorough."

Angela swept an arm out, gesturing toward a nearby hallway. "Be my guest," she said. "It's the last door on your left."

Nick thanked her, then they got to their feet and

moved down the hall. Rachel was relieved to be getting away from all those lifeless doll eyes.

Webber's room was spartan, with a spotless wooden floor, a neatly made bed, a dresser and a small desk that held a laptop computer.

Nick unplugged the computer from the wall. "We'll need to check his listings and his email. See if we can figure out who that buyer was. And I'll have Charlie pull his cell phone records."

Rachel nodded and went to the window, looking at the woods beyond. "We might want to check out there, too."

"Why?"

"She said he heard crying out there."

Nick sighed. "I thought we were past all that."

She turned. "Did Webber strike you as someone who was overly superstitious or out of his mind?"

"No."

"We're not talking about a ghost living in his basement. And I think it's safe to assume he was telling his wife the truth. I also think the killer didn't pick Webber at random, and it's possible that he or she was watching him from the woods. Trying to scare him. Which means there may be footprints out there. A cigarette butt. Something."

Nick considered this, nodded. "That makes sense. Let's take a look."

THE WOODS SEEMED LESS ominous in the light of day.

There was a simple beauty to the place that had Rachel thinking that Waterford Point wouldn't be a bad town to settle down in. She was a city girl, through and through, but a life without smog and traffic certainly had its appeal. Raising a child in a place surrounded by trees instead of concrete was probably not a terrible idea either.

Funny how thinking for two changed your perspective.

She supposed she'd be doing a lot of that now.

She and Nick spent several minutes searching the trees just outside the Webber house but didn't find anything useful, no sign that anyone had been out here at all.

But Rachel knew her instincts had been correct. Someone had stood right where she was standing now, late at night, watching Russ Webber through his bedroom window, planning his death.

She'd put money on it.

The question was why.

Why had someone gone to all the trouble of killing these people?

What was the story *beneath* the crime?

Rachel was sure this was a question that had been plaguing Nick for over three weeks now. And the answer to it was key. If they could figure out the motive for these murders, they'd be a long way toward identifying the perpetrator.

But maybe they needed to dig deeper. Maybe they should be going back much further than three and a half weeks. Solve *another* mystery before this one could be solved.

And with sudden clarity, Rachel knew exactly what had to be done.

Chapter Eight

"You realize, don't you, that you're investigating the wrong case?"

They were driving back toward town, and Nick was having a hard time concentrating on the road. He knew he could spend the drive going over a whole list of reasons why he shouldn't be attracted to Rachel, but it was already too late for that. These last couple hours with her had only strengthened what he'd been feeling ever since he met her.

"Did you hear me?"

He climbed out of his thoughts. "I'm sorry, what was that again?"

"You're investigating the wrong case," she said, emphasizing her words.

"What are you talking about? This is pretty much the only case I have, if you don't count Joey Bingham's missing skateboard and the couple dozen hysterical phone calls we get every day."

"I think it's pretty clear what the real connection between these deaths is."

He looked at her. "And what would that be?"

"It's right in front of us, and we can't ignore it simply because we don't believe in ghosts."

She was starting to sound like a broken record. And a slightly warped one at that. "We're back on Weeping Willow again?"

"The *person,* not the spirit."

Nick frowned. "I think you just lost me there."

She turned in her seat so that she was facing him. Broken record or not, she was beautiful. He hadn't met too many flawless women in his life. She undoubtedly had her share of imperfection, but they were invisible to the naked eye. Especially with the way the sunlight was playing in her hair.

"Thirty years ago," she said, "that girl and her foster parents were murdered. A murder that's never been solved and no one really seems to care about."

"They cared enough to turn it into a ghost story."

She shook her head. "That's only in the abstract. I don't know a lot about the case other than it's completely cold, but nobody seems to be rushing to reopen it."

"All right," Nick said. "But what's that got to do with the here and now?"

"Look at the victims. An attorney who comes to town to meet a mysterious client. A guy who was popular in high school and now lives with his mother. A woman who spent her days drinking her troubles away. And now a real estate agent who needed drugs and distraction to overcome his depression."

"I assume you're working toward some kind of point?"

"Think about it, Nick. Maybe these people were all witness to something. Maybe they know or saw who killed that poor girl and now the killer's been spooked somehow and he's decided to silence them."

Nick balked. "Three decades later?"

"Trust me," Rachel said, "I've seen crazier things happen. You know as well as I do that there's no statute of limitations on murder."

"So you really think her killer is still out there somewhere and he's worried he'll finally be caught?"

"I don't think it, I know it," she said. "I'm telling you, Nick, if you solve that girl's murder, you'll solve them all."

Nick mulled the idea over and had to admit that she could be right. Maybe Weeping Willow *was* the connection they'd been looking for, and he'd been so consumed with his theories about collective hysteria that he'd forgotten to look at the human side of the story.

"I feel like a fool," he said.

"Why?"

"I should have thought of this myself. I can't believe I looked right past it."

She touched his shoulder. "Don't beat yourself up too hard. You're right in the thick of it, remember? It's easier to get a broader picture when you're on the outside."

"I knew I should've brought the staties in, but I let Bill Burgess talk me out of it."

"Bill Burgess?"

"Our newly elected mayor," Nick said sourly. "He has a bit of a God complex. He's also a bigoted son of a…" He stopped, thinking there was no point in airing his petty annoyances. He was just angry with himself for his failure to see what Rachel had seen almost immediately.

Getting her input had obviously been the right move. In more ways than one.

"So what do you think?" she asked.

"I think you're right."

"Then we should probably get back to your office. Dig up those old files."

"That sounds like a good plan," he said. "But let's take a little side trip first."

"Where to?"

"Chaser's Ridge. The place where it all started."

CHASER'S RIDGE WAS A LARGE bluff that overlooked the town proper and the bay beyond. Like everywhere else in Waterford Point, it was dotted with Eastern pine.

Nestled in the trees were several expensive homes, and Rachel was starting to believe that this was much more than a simple tourist town. It was a retirement destination for those with money.

Nick took a winding road up the hillside and Rachel felt as if they were driving into an enchanted forest. Hopefully not the kind of place where unsuspecting children were stalked by evil witches.

"Almost there," he said.

They drove on for another half mile, then Nick spun the wheel and took a narrow dirt road into the trees. Several yards in, they came to a metal gate with a dilapidated sign that read No Trespassing.

Nick pulled to a stop. "We can walk from here."

"Where are you taking me?"

"You'll see." He moved up to the gate and pushed it open. "Somebody broke the lock years ago."

Then they continued up the road, which wound to the right and opened onto a good-size clearing.

There was a house in the middle of it.

Or what was left of one. The place had once been fairly large, but all that remained were its charred remnants—a blackened frame, a few burnt and broken pieces of furniture, an overturned stove, scorched and partially melted by fire.

There was a single wall still standing, its paint peeling, its surface pockmarked. Written across it in yellow spray paint were the words *Better Ded Then Red*.

The tagger obviously didn't know how to spell but the sentiment was clear.

As Rachel stared at the words, a dark energy washed over her, as if the place itself was warning her to turn around and never come back.

"That's a pretty strong statement," she said, pointing to the graffiti.

"The town isn't exactly overflowing with Native Americans," Nick told her. "And some people would just as soon we go back to the reservation."

"I take it this was the victim's house?"

He nodded. "The family still owns the property and has never bothered to sell it. So it just stands here as a reminder."

"And a pretty stark one at that," Rachel said.

They moved together toward the house, Rachel feeling a sudden chill. She hugged herself as they walked.

"Her name was Nadine Orono," Nick said. "Her foster parents were the Culbersons. I think they may have gone to the same church as my mother and father, but I can't be sure."

"How old were you when it happened?"

"Almost four. I remember it because my mother got very upset. Not so much because they knew the Culbersons—although I'm sure that was part of it—but because Nadine was originally from Indian Island, just like my mother. It always cuts a little deeper when you see one of your own go down." He gestured to the graffiti on the wall. "Especially like this."

"What else do you remember?" Rachel asked.

"Not much. I was too interested in watching cartoons to pay much attention. But I do remember how the legend of the girl's ghost grew over the years. Whenever anything bad happened around here, the kids would blame it on Weeping Willow. She became a convenient tool for parents, too, warning their children to toe the line or the ghost would come after them."

"I'm sure *that* worked."

He shrugged. "I was always taught that spirits aren't something to be feared, so it never made a whole lot of sense to me."

He moved closer to the house now and got down

on his haunches. Grabbing a handful of dirt, he let it sift though his fingers.

Rachel remembered this from the crime scene. "What are you doing?"

He opened his eyes. "It's something my grandfather always did. In my culture, the land is as much a part of the universe as the people and animals who inhabit it. We consider the earth a gift, not a possession."

"I think I can agree with that."

"My grandfather used to say that this was his way of speaking to the land, asking for its secrets." He got to his feet. "I have no idea if he ever got an answer. I never have."

"Not even now?"

He shook his head. "But, call me crazy, I *do* feel a restlessness here. As if the spirit of that poor girl wants to be set free."

"Not crazy at all," Rachel said. "I feel something, too. Although I'm not sure it's anything good."

"Nothing about this case is good."

They went back to his cruiser. As they climbed in, Nick looked at her with a quiet fire in his eyes. "You were right. Nadine Orono's murder has become a footnote in this town. I can see that even more clearly now."

"Then I guess we'd better change that."

Their gazes locked for a moment, then he turned and started the engine. He glanced at her again, as if he wanted to say something more but was holding back.

"What is it?" she asked.

Nick hesitated. "Just that I'm glad we're working together. I'm sorry I wasn't more receptive last night."

"You already apologized for that."

He shrugged. "It doesn't hurt to say it again. And I have to be honest with you, Rachel. There's something about you that..." He stopped himself.

"That what?"

She thought she knew where he was going with this and her heart accelerated.

But he shook his head again. "Let's just concentrate on Nadine."

Then he put the car in gear and started to drive.

Chapter Nine

They were almost to the bottom of the hill when the excitement started.

Nick's radio squawked. "Nick, this is Charlie. What's your twenty?"

He sounded a little frantic. Nick picked up the mic and clicked it on. "I'm just coming off Chaser's Ridge. What's up?"

"You've got a runner coming your way. Try to intercept."

"Roger," Nick said. "Who is it?"

"Vern Robinson. He decided to tie one on a little early today and came into town waving a gun. Kept babbling on about how Weeping Willow's coming after him."

"What?"

"He's drunk, Nick, and he's not making much sense. But when I tried to confront him, he waved his gun at me, then grabbed Mavis Beacham's car and took off. You know how she's always leaving the keys in that thing."

They were at the bottom of the hill now, just in time to see an old Chevy streak by, going what Rachel thought had to be at least ninety miles an hour.

"I see him," Nick said into the radio. "I'm in pursuit." He turned to Rachel. "You better jump out now."

Rachel felt her adrenaline rise. "What are you talking about?"

"This could get a little crazy."

"So you want me stand out here in the middle of nowhere while you have all the fun? We're partners now, remember?"

"I'm serious, Rachel."

"Just drive," she said.

He looked at her with a mix of surprise and fascination, then flipped a switch on the dash.

Rachel winced as the siren assaulted her ears, then braced herself as the car shot forward, pulling onto the main thoroughfare.

The road ahead was empty, which wasn't surprising considering how fast the guy in the Chevy had been going.

"Hold on," Nick said, then goosed the gas pedal, picking up speed, the cruiser barely breaking a sweat.

And neither was Nick.

Rachel, on the other hand, was starting to regret her decision to stay in the car. Her instinct for survival kicked in and panic started to rise in her throat. Her heart was pounding so hard she thought it might burst through her chest.

Then she saw the Chevy up ahead, smoke billowing out of its tailpipe as it slowed slightly, taking a sharp curve.

"There he is!" she said, stating the obvious.

But Nick wasn't paying any attention. All of his concentration was centered on driving. He kept his hands steady on the wheel as he worked the gas pedal like a pro, slowing only slightly as they moved into the curve behind the Chevy.

The centrifugal force knocked Rachel against the door, and she clambered for the hand brace mounted above it, hanging on for dear life.

Now the Chevy was only a few yards ahead. The driver had to have heard the siren behind him but he didn't waver, didn't show any sign of pulling over.

Nick flipped a switch on the dash and grabbed his radio mic.

"Vern, this is Nick Chavaree. Pull your car over, right now."

Nick's voice blasted out over a loudspeaker but good old Vern didn't slow down.

"Come on, Vern. Stop your car right—"

The driver of the Chevy suddenly slammed on his brakes, his tires screeching beneath him.

Nick dropped the mic, grabbed the wheel with both hands and hit his own brakes, swerving to the other side of the road to prevent an impact.

After a long, loud skid—Rachel's heart jumping up into her throat—the cruiser came to a stop not ten feet away from the Chevy.

Nick cranked the hand brake and jumped out. Vern was already out of his car and running across a wide green field. His gait was loping and wild and he was carrying a gun in his right hand.

Nick leaned in.

"Stay here and keep your head down," he told her, then unsnapped his holster and took off after Vern.

Rachel heard more sirens in the distance and knew that Charlie and the other deputies would be here soon. Staying low in her seat, she peeked out the window as Nick ran across the field, moving with the grace and speed of a natural athlete.

He was almost on top of him, when Vern cried out and wheeled around, raising the gun.

Rachel's heart stopped.

"Stay away from me, Nick! I don't trust you. I don't trust any of you."

"What are you talking about, Vern? Put the gun down."

"You know everything, don't you? You know exactly what happened. *She* told you. She told you everything."

Nick said something in response, but his voice was drowned out as three deputy's cruisers came tearing around the curve, their sirens blaring.

Nick's gun was still in its holster, his hands raised as Vern waved his own gun in threat.

But Nick didn't flinch. Didn't move. And Rachel had never seen anything like it.

The cruisers came to a sudden screeching halt, then the sirens went silent as Charlie and two other deputies jumped out, ripping their weapons free.

Charlie moved to the edge of the field and gripped his gun with both hands, going into the standard shooting stance. "Vern Robinson, you'd better put that gun down right now or I'll blow you ten ways to Sunday."

"You're all in it together," Vern shouted. "You and Weeping Willow."

"Easy, Vern," Nick said. "Just take it easy and we can talk about this. But you have to put the gun down first."

"This all my fault," Vern cried. "I'm the reason those people are dead. It was my idea."

"Vern, you're drunk. You know you're drunk. And when we're drunk, we do crazy things. So what do you say you put the gun down and we can go back to the station and you tell us whatever it is that's on your mind. Anything you want."

Vern seemed to calm a little. Rachel was still trying to wrap her head around the fact that Nick was standing there without protection, without even lowering his hand toward his holster.

She got the feeling that this wasn't his first time to the rodeo.

"Come on, Vern, if you don't do what I tell you, ol' Charlie there's gonna have to shoot. And neither one of us wants that, right?"

Vern was wobbling now, starting to lower the gun, his eyes glazed. He looked as if he was about to give in. Nick's body began to relax a little.

But then, suddenly, something shifted in Vern's eyes and he jerked the gun up again. "I don't trust a single one of you," he said.

He pointed the gun at Nick, and just as he was about to squeeze the trigger, Rachel screamed—

—and a shot rang out.

Charlie's shot.

Vern tumbled backward into the grass, his gun flying. Then Nick ran to him, crouching over him as Charlie and one of the deputies bolted across the field.

Another deputy hung back and radioed for an ambulance as Rachel scrambled out of the cruiser and crossed the field.

Charlie looked up sharply as she approached. "What the heck are *you* doing here?"

"She's with me," Nick said.

"But I thought—"

"Stow it, Charlie. Just help me tend to Vern."

"Is he dead?" Rachel asked.

Nick shook his head. "Shoulder wound. Charlie's an expert shot. Good man to have in a pinch."

"What was he talking about? All that stuff about this being all his fault?"

Nick was checking the wound. "Your guess is as good as mine. But whatever it was, I have a feeling it's gonna be a while before we find out. Condition of this shoulder, he's looking at a week minimum in the hospital."

"You think he really has something to do with the Weeping Willow case?"

"He's drunk," Charlie said. "Even sober he doesn't make much sense."

Rachel stared at Vern's broken form and wondered how he fit into the equation.

One thing was for sure: the longer she stayed here, the more complicated Waterford Point got.

Chapter Ten

"Looks to me like we've got ourselves a suspect," Bill Burgess said.

Nick was incredulous. "Vern?"

Burgess indicated the pages in his hand. "I had your secretary fax me Charlie Tevis's initial report. He says Vern confessed."

They were standing in the reception area of the mayor's office. Waterford Point's city hall was nothing more than a large Victorian mansion located at the center of town, about two blocks west of the sheriff's building.

Nick had been summoned here shortly after they'd gotten Vern Robinson squared away at the hospital. He'd brought Rachel along with him.

Rachel had remained seated as Nick rose to greet Burgess, but she hadn't escaped Burgess's eye. And Nick knew the man liked what he saw, which only heightened his annoyance.

"I don't know what report you were reading," he said, "but Vern didn't confess to anything."

Burgess looked down at the piece of paper in his hand. Charlie had prepared the report in record time, but then he'd always been efficient.

"'It's all my fault,'" Burgess read. "'I'm the reason those people are dead. It was my idea.'" He looked up at Nick again. "That doesn't sound like a confession to you?"

"I'll admit it sounds like somebody who has something on his mind, but I wouldn't call it a confession."

"Well, that's exactly what it is," Burgess insisted. "And you're gonna arrest this man and take the case to the county prosecutor."

"Not until I've had a chance to talk to him."

"So what's stopping you?"

"You read the report, didn't you? Or did your whole world come to a halt when you got to Vern's so-called confession?"

"I don't need any attitude, Nick. Either fill me in or I'll find somebody else who will." He gestured to Rachel. "Maybe your cute little girlfriend here."

Rachel eyed him dully and Nick said, "Leave her out of it. Vern's in the O.R. Doctor says he's in worse condition than we thought and he may not make it through surgery."

"Doesn't mean we can't file charges anyway."

"Based on what?"

"Based on what I've read here. It's enough for me."

Nick tried to contain his fury. "Well, it's not enough for *me*."

"What do you want, Chavaree? This is our chance to set everyone's mind at ease. Let them know the killer's been caught and they can breathe easy and go about their business."

"Do you for one minute think Vern Robinson is capable of killing anyone?"

Burgess's eyes were burning now. He didn't like his authority being questioned. "I think every single one of us is capable of it. You were in Afghanistan, right? I'm sure you must've put your war paint on once or twice, bagged a few bad guys."

Nick gritted his teeth and tried to restrain himself. "You're lucky I'm a tolerant man, Bill."

"Why's that?"

"Because if I weren't, I'd be ripping you apart right about now."

Burgess took a step back. "Is that a threat?"

"Consider it a warning," Nick said. "Because if you keep saying things like that, I may have to go native and start kicking your—"

"You can't talk to me that way. I'm the *mayor* of this town."

"Well, good for you. Throw in a couple bucks, you'll still only be worth about fifty cents."

Burgess blinked at him but Nick didn't give him a chance to search for a suitable response. Turning to Rachel, he said, "Let's get out of here."

They started toward the exit and Burgess finally found his voice. "You're fired, Chavaree. You got that?"

"Tell it to the city council."

"You'd better turn in your gun and badge, kemos-abe. Right now."

Nick ignored him and they went out the door.

"THIS PLACE JUST GETS more and more interesting," Rachel said as they headed up the block toward the sheriff's office.

Nick gave her a look. "We must have different definitions of that word. There's nothing less interesting than small-town politics."

"It's the storyteller in me. Conflict makes for good drama. Along with colorful characters."

"Is that what I am to you? A colorful character?"

"I was thinking more of your mayor. I've seen my

share of overbearing, officious idiots in my time, but he may just win the prize."

"Now *that's* a definition we can agree on."

Rachel laughed. "You don't seem very concerned for a man who's just lost his job."

"He can't fire me unless the city council signs off on it, and they like him even less than I do."

"So how did he manage to get elected?"

"Sheer willpower," Nick said.

"Well, Sheriff, I've gotta say I was pretty impressed with the way you stood up to him."

Nick gave her an imaginary tip of the hat. "Thank you kindly, ma'am."

She laughed again. "I was also impressed with the way you handled Vern Robinson in that field today. Not too many people would go up against an armed man like that and not draw their weapon."

Nick shrugged. "Vern's actually a puppy dog. And I knew Charlie was backing me up."

"It still took a lot of nerve and you know it. And I can tell by those scars on your chest that you're no stranger to violence, so you knew exactly what was at stake."

Nick stopped in his tracks, arched an eyebrow at her. "I guess I wasn't the only one with roving eyes this morning."

Rachel felt herself starting to flush. "We don't need to talk about that."

"Maybe we should," Nick said.

"What do you want to do, compare cup sizes? I think I've probably got you beat in that department."

"Trust me, that's a battle I don't mind losing. And since I'm all riled up after my little spat with Burgess, I figure I might as well be completely straight with you."

"Meaning what?"

Those intense brown eyes of his locked on to her gaze. "I don't know if you've got a husband or a boyfriend or what's going on in your personal life. But I like you, Rachel. I like you a lot. Matter of fact, I can't stop thinking about you. Or looking at you."

Rachel's heart kicked up a notch. "You barely know me."

"But I'm *getting* to know you and I like everything I see."

Without meaning to, Rachel thought about Dan. He'd liked everything he saw, too. Until he didn't.

And it had been the same for her.

"I appreciate that," she said. "But I'm not really interested in being anyone's few and far between."

"It's not like that."

"Oh? How do you know?"

"Same way you do."

She drew back slightly. "That's pretty presumptuous."

"Come on, Rachel, are you telling me you don't feel it? There's something between us."

She couldn't deny it. She'd been trying to fight it off ever since she'd met him, but that didn't mean they were destined to be soul mates any more than she and Dan had been.

Besides, Nick didn't know she was pregnant. And that was a game changer.

"Look," she said, "I'd be lying if I didn't admit I'm attracted to you. I mean, look at you, any woman would be."

"I'm not talking about any woman. Or what's on the surface."

The look on his face made Rachel want to melt into his arms at that very moment.

But she resisted.

She had to keep reminding herself that they'd known each other less than a day. How could any kind of solid relationship be built on that?

"I'm sorry, Nick, I really am. But this is a bad time for me. I've got too much going on in my life. Getting involved with someone just isn't the kind of complication I need right now. I hope you understand."

He said nothing for a long moment.

She could see that he was disappointed and she hated that she'd hurt him. She had a knot in her stomach because of it.

Then he nodded. "I had to give it a shot," he said. "But you're right. And once again I feel like an idiot."

"No…" She grabbed his hand. The feel of his skin against hers was electric. "You're not an idiot at all. I told you, this just isn't the right time for me."

And if she didn't let go of him, immediately, she might change her mind.

But then he pulled away.

"All right," he said. "Fair enough. I hope this doesn't mean it'll be awkward between us. That we can still work together."

"I won't let it be if you won't."

But in truth, it already was. And they both knew it. But they were grown-ups, too, and growns-ups lied to each other all the time.

"Then let's get back to work," Nick said.

She tried not to think about the pain she'd caused him. "Okay, what's next?"

"Back to our original plan. We dig up the files on Nadine Orono."

Chapter Eleven

The Waterford Point sheriff's department wasn't much to look at. The building was a drab gray and had a prefab feel that failed to capture a sense of New England like the rest of the town. It could easily have been picked up and transported whole from California's San Fernando Valley, along with all the personality—or lack thereof—that went with it.

Rachel shuddered slightly. It even reminded her of the police substation she'd been taken to after Emit Lattimore attacked her.

The archives were located in the basement, a narrow, dank room lit only by a single fluorescent bulb that made their skin look a little green.

It was immediately obvious to Rachel that the room was rarely used. Metal shelves lined the walls with old, dilapidated bank boxes piled high atop them, carrying records of every assault, every break-in, every traffic stop that had been handled by the department over the last hundred years or so.

At the center of the room was a line of file cabinets with more boxes piled on top of them, and it amazed Rachel that a town the size of Waterford Point could have so much crime.

That is, if jaywalking really counted as a crime.

"You sure you want to do this?" Charlie Tevis asked as they navigated the steps.

"We think the girl's murder might be the connection we're looking for," Nick told him.

"I thought you didn't believe in ghosts?"

"I don't," Nick said, then quickly filled him in on Rachel's idea.

Charlie nodded, gesturing to the disarray. "Good luck finding anything in this mess."

Rachel stared at the piles of boxes. "Don't you ever purge these things?"

Charlie snorted. "That's what I wanted to know when I got here a couple years ago. Even volunteered to do the purging."

"So what happened?"

"After about three hours of frustration, I gave up and decided to keep my trap shut."

"So are you telling me we're in needle-and-haystack territory?"

"More like a crapshoot. Sometimes you get lucky, sometimes you don't."

"I'm not even going to ask how it got this way."

"Neither one of us could tell you," Nick said. "We inherited this mess and nobody has the time or energy to clean it up."

"So is it too much to expect Nadine's case file to be alphabetized?"

Nick and Charlie both laughed.

"I'm afraid we're in this for the long haul," Nick told her. "But like Charlie said, maybe we'll get lucky."

THEY DIDN'T.

The most recent cases—the ones that had been stored down here after Nick took over the sheriff's position—were in neat alphabetical order in the file cabinets in the center of the room.

But anything beyond the past five years was stuffed haphazardly into one of the boxes, sometimes arranged by date, sometimes by name, sometimes by category of crime and sometimes with no rhyme or reason at all. Finding any consistency in the system was an exercise in deep frustration.

No wonder Nadine Orono's case had never been reopened.

About two hours in, Charlie threw his hands up

and said he'd had enough. His vision was getting blurry.

Nick tried to stop him as he headed up the steps but Charlie didn't listen.

"You can fire me if you want to. But I'm not spending another minute down here."

When he was gone, Rachel and Nick kept at it, each pulling another box off the shelf.

When Rachel finished browsing through the hundred or so files stuffed inside hers, she said, "We're not going to find it, are we?"

"Aren't you the optimist."

"Nobody ever thought to transfer this stuff to a computer?"

"Are you volunteering?"

"Ha," she said. "Not likely."

Shoving the box aside, she moved to a new shelf and reached for one of the bank boxes on top. But as she pulled on it, she felt something shift.

Nick shouted, "Look out!"

An avalanche tumbled toward her. Just as she thought she was about to get flattened, she felt hands on her waist, yanking her away.

She and Nick tumbled backward onto the floor, Nick taking the brunt of the impact as Rachel landed on top of him.

Several of the boxes crashed around them, at least

two of them ripping open, scattering files all over the place.

When the dust cleared, Nick said, "Are you okay?"

"Me? What about you? You got the worst of it."

He laughed. "I'm not complaining."

He still had his arms around her. They were solid, well muscled, steady—and despite her better instincts, Rachel didn't want to move. Wanted to stay like this for as long as possible.

He shifted beneath her and she thought he was about to push her off him, when he surprised her by brushing his lips against her neck.

A stutter of electricity shot through her, and she didn't resist, wouldn't even *dream* of resisting.

"I hope I'm not being too presumptuous," he murmured. "This not being the right time and all."

Then his hands were moving, one of them reaching up to touch the breast he'd had a peek at this morning. As she turned in his arms, he lifted his head toward hers and kissed her.

She felt his tongue brush against her teeth and invited it in, the current of energy inside her widening… deepening…spreading….

And in that moment, she wanted him more than anyone she'd ever wanted before.

This was so much more than that elusive spark she

was always hoping for. This was an all-out assault on every nerve ending in her body. A pleasure so deep and so satisfying that she could barely contain herself.

And this from only a *kiss*...

It killed her to do it, but she gently pulled away from him. "We're making a mistake, you know."

"The best mistake I've ever made," he told her, then pulled her close and kissed her again.

THEY BARELY HAD THEIR CLOTHES buttoned when the door at the top of the stairs flew open and Charlie moved down the steps toward them.

"You two aren't gonna believe this," he said. Then he suddenly stopped in his tracks and squinted at them. "What's going on down here?"

Rachel felt herself redden. Tried to smooth her hair.

Nick stood beside her, snapping on his gun belt, trying his best to look official and failing miserably. She wasn't sure, but she thought he had a trace of a smile on his face.

The bonehead.

But Charlie was oblivious to all this. His gaze was fixed on the overturned boxes and the files scattered across the floor.

"Looks like you two had an accident," he said. "Everybody okay?"

Now Nick was smiling, trying hard to stifle it, and Rachel wanted to put an elbow in his ribs.

"We're fine," he said. "Just took a bit of a tumble."

He shot Rachel a knowing glance and despite herself, she felt her own smile coming on and had to use every bit of the strength she had left to prevent it from surfacing.

So much for keeping things professional.

"You gotta be careful down here," Charlie said. "This place is a house of cards."

Rachel moved toward him, trying to cover her embarrassment. "What was it you wanted to tell us?"

"I just remembered that when I was down here to purge the files, I took a box upstairs with me and stuck it in my office closet." He smiled and brought a folder out from behind his back, waving it at them. "You'll never guess whose case file I found."

"You've gotta be kidding me," Rachel said.

"I kid you not. Nadine Orono Culberson." He tossed the file to Nick. "Too bad you two had to waste all that time down here."

Then he looked at them both, a bit of a twinkle in his eyes.

Chapter Twelve

Nadine Orono's file was a disappointment.

Rachel wasn't sure what she'd been hoping to find, but the thing was as thin as an accident report and probably less informative.

There was an arson investigator's summary that ran only two pages long, a couple of faded snapshots of the burned-down house, some autopsy and crime scene photos of the bodies—or what was left of them, a few brief statements by the first responders and the neighbor who had discovered the blaze and a follow-up sheet with the details on Nadine's foster parents, including the adoption papers they'd recently filed.

In other words, busy work. Without much follow-through.

There were a few additional witness statements taken from the Jefferson High principal, Nadine's teachers and a couple high school students who had known her. None of them had much to offer. It was clear from the interviews that their involvement with the girl had been peripheral at best, largely restricted to the classroom.

The thing that struck Rachel, however, was that Nadine had only been fifteen years old when she died. She'd barely had a chance to live.

Or love.

Or be loved.

Rachel sighed and leaned back in her chair. "Such a shame," she said. "And no wonder this case was never solved. You ask me, nobody really tried."

They were sitting at a conference table in a windowless room. Nick had pulled his chair up close, looking at the file over her shoulder. She could feel his warmth against her back, and she kept replaying their brief encounter in the archive room through her mind.

We're making a mistake, you know.

The best mistake I've ever made.

It certainly hadn't been the most romantic location for their first time together, but in those few moments, Nick had taken her places she'd never been before.

The problem was that she was completely distracted now, when she should be concentrating.

She couldn't help wondering what those moments had meant. She and Nick hadn't had a chance to talk since Charlie barged in and she had a lot questions that needed to be answered.

The best mistake I ever made.

Had it been a mistake?

The moment had been quick and passionate and had definitely fulfilled an urge that had been boiling up inside of both of them.

But what now?

They knew too little about each other to consider it something serious. Yet Rachel couldn't stop thinking about it. She wasn't a slam-bam-thank-you-ma'am kind of girl.

"What about these adoption papers?" Nick said, interrupting her thoughts. He pulled them out and placed them atop the small stack in front of her.

"What about them?"

He pointed to a case summary at the bottom of the page. "Says here that Nadine had a sixteen-year-old brother."

She nodded. "I saw that."

Nadine's birth parents were full-blooded Penobscot Indians. They had been living away from the reservation when they were killed, and Nadine and her brother immediately went into foster care.

Unfortunately, the two had been split up. Nadine was sent to live with the Culbersons, while her brother, Samuel, went to another family in New Hampshire.

"Maybe they kept in contact," Nick said. "She may have had a lot to say in her letters and phone calls. Something that would have helped the investigation."

"I don't see any statements from him."

"Because you're right—nobody really tried. The investigating officer probably didn't think it was worth the time and effort to track him down." He scraped his chair back and got to his feet.

"Where are you going?"

"I think I'll do what that IO should've done thirty years ago. Run this guy's name through the databases, see what I get."

"You plan on talking to him?"

"I don't see how it could hurt," Nick said.

NICK WAS HAPPY to be in front of a computer. He was relieved to have all the files he needed at his fingertips, requiring no more storage space than a half-dozen hard drives.

Not that he was complaining. If that archive room wasn't such a disaster, his rendezvous with Rachel wouldn't have happened.

Not today, at least.

And not in quite that way.

Nick firmly believed that much of what happens to us in this world depends on fate, and he knew in his gut that Rachel was part of his. He wasn't able to quantify this feeling and he'd never been much on self-analysis, but his instincts had always been pretty reliable.

Nick hadn't had that many relationships in his life. There was Jennifer in high school and Elise in college, yet neither of them had given him that sense of completion he longed for. After he was done with school, he'd had a few quick, unsatisfying dalliances that didn't go much beyond hello and goodbye, and he'd almost become convinced that he was destined to spend his life as a monk.

The detour to Afghanistan certainly hadn't helped.

Yet Afghanistan, oddly enough, was where he first came across one of Rachel's books. It was called *Broken Valentine*, the story of a marriage gone criminally sour. He'd found it in a pile of donated reading material at the base camp, saw her photo on the back and couldn't resist.

He remembered that after he'd read the book—which had been well written and riveting—he had checked her bio, looked at the photo again and thought, why don't I ever meet women like this?

It was just one of those things you say to yourself

and dismiss the moment you say it, never dreaming it might one day have some significance.

Yet there Rachel was, nearly six years—and five books—later, sitting in the next room. And only a few moments before, he'd held her in his arms.

And then some.

If that wasn't fate, what was it?

The computer beeped and Nick blinked, pulling himself out of his reverie. He had done an advanced meta-search through several law enforcement databases, hoping to get a hit on Samuel Orono, and he didn't have to wait long.

He got several hits, in fact, all of them originating out of Larchmont, New Hampshire, a city that had actually gotten around to digitizing its older case files. All but one of those hits had originated over two decades ago, when Samuel Joseph Orono was still a young man.

There were two minor thefts, a misdemeanor drunk and disorderly, a pot charge and two speeding tickets. Then there was nothing until about three years ago, when Orono filed to have the two thefts expunged from his record.

Nick pulled the application up and was surprised to discover that his address was listed as Indian Island. He'd moved back to Maine and was staying at the reservation.

There was a phone number listed. Nick grabbed the receiver on his desk and dialed.

After two rings, a woman answered, "Hello?"

"Hi, I'm looking for Samuel Joseph Orono."

There was a pause. "I'm afraid you've got the wrong number."

"There's nobody named Samuel there?"

"No," she said. "This is a cell phone. But I only got this number a few months ago, so maybe he gave it up."

Nick thanked her and cradled the receiver.

If it was a cell phone number, then it wasn't attached to a specific address, so Orono could still be living on Indian Island.

"Any luck?"

Nick turned to find Rachel standing in his office doorway, looking tired yet radiant. He wished he could put all this craziness aside and pull her into his arms again.

"I've got an address but I'm not sure how current it is. The phone number was a bust."

She nodded, but he could see that her mind was elsewhere. "We need to talk, Nick."

He didn't like the sound of that. In his world, such words were code for "you're about to be dumped." Which didn't make a whole lot of sense considering they'd barely even started this thing.

She closed door behind her and sat in a chair in front of his desk.

"There's something you need to know about me," she said.

"I'd like to know as much as I can."

He waited as she gathered herself and tried to figure out how to say what she had to say. "Despite being impulsive when it comes to my work, I don't rush into things on the emotional front."

"Neither do I," he said.

"So then what exactly happened back there? I mean, don't get me wrong, I loved every second of it—but did it mean anything? Or was it just something we can grin about when we're bragging to our friends?"

"I don't kiss and tell, if that's what you're afraid of."

Rachel sighed and he could see by her look that he'd completely missed the point.

"I told you outside that I'm not ready to get involved. There are just too many things going on in my life and I have to—"

"Like the baby?"

She paused and looked at him. Then the realization struck her. "Let me guess…Maddie?"

"The one and only. But I'm not blind and I think I would've figured it out sooner or later."

"And it doesn't bother you?"

Nick shook his head. "You can't scare me away, Rachel, if that's what you're hoping to do. You're obviously conflicted about all of this and I understand that. But I meant what I said outside. There's something between us, and I don't see it going away anytime soon."

Rachel stared at her hands. "But that's the problem, Nick. I've already been through this once. Rushing into something only to see it fall apart. I don't want that to happen again."

"It's like Charlie said. Sometimes you get lucky, sometimes you don't. And I guess I'm feeling pretty lucky right now."

"But what if you're wrong?"

Nick leaned back in his chair. He could feel her trepidation.

"Look," he said. "I don't want to pressure you into anything. You say you don't like to rush, then we take it slow. See where it goes."

She was silent, still looking at her hands. Then she lifted her head and there were tears in her eyes.

"You're in the wrong profession, you know that? You should've been a salesman."

"So does that mean you're buying?"

She smiled now, gave him a small laugh. "Sampling," she said. "Still sampling."

Chapter Thirteen

The first thing she saw was Princess Watahwaso's Teepee.

It was at least thirty feet tall and looked like a giant, upside-down, red-and-white sugar cone. Hanging above the door was a large American flag.

The teepee stood on the left side of the road as Nick and Rachel drove the bridge over the Penobscot River onto Indian Island.

Rachel was behind the wheel. They had taken her rental across on the ferry and traveled an hour and a half up Bangor Road to get here.

Back at the office, Nick had tried and failed to find a new phone number for Samuel Orono. So, using the address from Nadine's case file, they decided to see if they could track him down to speak to him in person.

The reservation, like Waterford Point, was beautiful. Full of lush green trees, particularly white birch and brown ash, which Nick said was used to weave baskets. Basket weaving had a long history among the Penawahpskewi—or Penobscot Indians—dating back to a time when they were the only inhabitants on the riverside.

"There's an old Penawahpskewi folktale," Nick told her, "about how the river came to be."

They were traveling along Down Street, a single-lane road. Nick seemed to be lost in a memory and his voice had a faraway quality to it.

"The story goes that the Penawahpskewi were dying because a monster frog was sucking up all the water in the area and refused to give them any. Then the great spirit Gluskabe came along and told the frog that the water, like the land around them, was meant to be shared.

"But the frog still refused to share it, so Gluskabe toppled a birch tree and killed the monster, forcing all the water out of its body. And the Penobscot River was formed."

"Sounds like something your grandfather must have told you."

Nick nodded. "We came here a lot when I was kid. Most of my mother's family is here."

"Was it tough for her to be living away from home?"

"She left when she was pretty young. Was nineteen

when she married my father. I'm sure she must have missed it, but she loved Waterford Point, too. And I doubt it was as tough for her as it was for Nadine Orono."

They continued along the road, passing a wooden building that housed the Penobscot Nation Museum, then took a right at Bridge Street, crossing the river again until they came to Wabanaki Way.

They soon found themselves in the middle of the business district, with a large bingo palace on their right and a police and fire station to the left.

Nick gestured for Rachel to pull into the police station.

"We need to let them know what we're up to," he said. "The reservation has its own laws and government. We don't want to step on anyone's toes."

As Rachel found a spot out front, a hybrid SUV glided up next to them and a guy in a uniform who, from a distance, could have been Nick's twin, climbed out and walked over to his window.

Nick rolled it down and the other man leaned in. "Well, well, cuz, long time no see. What you brings you here?"

"Business, unfortunately."

"Business?"

"We're here to interview a witness. Assuming he still lives here."

The other man looked at Rachel. "And who's we?"

Nick quickly introduced them, telling Rachel that this was his cousin, Thomas Chavaree. Thomas reached through the window and they shook hands.

"Wish I had a partner looked like you," he said, holding on a little longer than he needed to. "I'm stuck with a fat guy who can't keep mustard off his shirt."

He let go and returned his gaze to Nick. "So who's this witness you're looking for?"

"Guy named Samuel Orono."

Thomas nodded. "You're in luck. He still lives here. Moved into his grandparents' old house a couple years back. Over on Bear Ridge Road."

Nick had told Rachel that there were only about five hundred or so residents on the reservation, most of whom had lived here for decades.

"Thanks, Tom. You mind letting the powers that be know where we're headed?"

"Will do. But don't think you can get out of here without a visit to the family. Early dinner tonight." He flashed a smile at Rachel. "And bring your partner."

Then he patted the roof of the car and headed into the station.

Rachel watched him go. "Seems like a nice guy."

"Don't stare too hard."

She laughed. "I thought I had double vision for minute there."

"Look but don't touch," Nick said. "In fact, don't even look."

She laughed again and put the car in reverse.

THE ORONO HOUSE WAS OLD and run-down and seriously in need of some loving care. There was a mangy dog sitting on the porch out front, his eyes following them as Nick and Rachel climbed out of her car and headed for the steps.

"He looks harmless enough," Nick said.

"So did you."

They moved together up the steps to a dilapidated screen door. The dog didn't move.

Nick was about to knock when a voice to their right said, "Nobody home."

They turned with a start.

There was a guy in his mid-forties slumped low in a chair in the corner of the porch. He wore a cowboy hat tilted toward his nose to shade his face. He was Native American, his plaid shirt a bit too tight, accentuating a good-size paunch.

"Who you lookin' for?" he asked.

Nick moved toward him and held out a hand to shake. "Mr. Orono?"

"That's right," he said, ignoring Nick's hand. "I

see you're law enforcement, but not from around here. What do you want?"

"We're from Waterford Point. We're here to talk to you about your sister."

Orono titled his hat back and sat up. "You sure took your time, didn't you?"

"MY GRANDPARENTS WERE dirt-poor," Orono said. "Yet after our parents were killed, they wanted to take us in anyway. But we were off the reservation and child protective services figured we'd be better off in foster homes." He snorted. "Guess nobody could ever accuse the state of having good ideas."

They were in Orono's living room now, which was full of furniture that looked like it had been there for several decades. The sofa was covered with faded, multicolored blankets, and the throw rug beneath Rachel's feet was so worn it nearly had holes in it.

Orono had pulled some sodas from the refrigerator and passed them around.

"Did you and Nadine ever communicate?" Rachel asked.

He plopped into a scuffed and faded easy chair. "At first she wrote me practically every day. Just short little notes telling me how miserable she was."

"In what way?"

He shrugged. "The usual stuff. She didn't like

her foster parents much. Too many rules. The kids at school thought she was a dweeb. Stuff like that."

"Did she mention any kids in particular?" Nick asked. "Anyone who may have threatened her?"

"Never anything specific. Just that they'd laugh at her in gym class and throw food at her in the cafeteria."

Rachel shook her head in disgust. "Kids can be so cruel."

"Especially when you don't look or act like them. And sometimes those kids don't grow up."

Rachel thought of Mayor Burgess and his "kemosabe" crack at Nick. Now *there* was a man whose growth was seriously stunted.

Orono took a sip of his soda. "I kept getting letters from her, two to three times a month after that. But then they suddenly stopped."

"And you didn't wonder why?" Nick asked.

"Of course I did. I wrote her a couple times asking what was up, and she finally wrote me back. Last letter I ever got from her."

"What did it say?"

"She said she'd made a friend. Which to my mind translated to boyfriend and was why she was suddenly too busy to write."

Rachel felt her pulse accelerate. "Did she say who it was?"

Orono shook his head. "But she was into the guy, I can tell you that much. You want me to show it to you?"

"By all means," Nick said.

Orono drained his soda, then lifted himself out of the easy chair and disappeared through a doorway. He came back a moment later carrying a worn cardboard shoe box. He had the lid off and was digging around inside. When he found what he was looking for, he handed it to Rachel.

She opened the envelope, took out a single page and unfolded it.

It was written with a delicate pen. Curlicue letters with a heart dotting the *i* in Nadine.

Rachel quietly read the letter and felt her heart start to melt.

The words were brief and to the point. She was still being harassed but school was better now that she had a friend. Someone she called her "little bird."

She told Orono that she probably wouldn't be writing as much, but she still loved him and thought of him every day.

She ended the letter with a short poem. Rachel read it aloud:

"Broken, beaten and abused,

My cries were never heard

Until they rose into the sky

And found a little bird
I never knew what joy could be
Until that fateful day
He came to me on silver wings
And took my pain away."

So Nadine had found love, Rachel thought. She'd known the joy of it. That feeling that envelopes you and lifts you skyward. Makes you believe you can conquer the world.

But what had gone wrong?

And was her "little bird" responsible?

None of the witnesses had claimed to be her boyfriend, so who was this bird and why hadn't he come forward?

It didn't make much sense unless he was the one who had killed her.

And her foster parents.

And lit their house on fire.

Rachel looked up from the letter and saw that Orono had tears in his eyes. The wounds were old yet still fresh.

"You sure you don't have any idea who she was writing about?" Rachel asked. "This 'little bird'?"

"Not a clue," he said. "And the first time I read that poem, I almost gagged. Thought it had to be the sappiest thing I'd ever seen." His gaze shifted to the floor. "Shows you what an insensitive jerk I am."

"You didn't know what would happen, Mr. Orono. You couldn't know."

He nodded solemnly. "That's what I keep telling myself." Then he looked up again. "So what's this all about anyway? Why now? I contacted the Waterford Point sheriff's office almost three decades ago but nobody bothered to return my calls."

"We're trying to rectify that," Nick said.

"But why do you care all of a sudden? Is it because of you?"

He looked pointedly at Nick. He obviously didn't know about the recent murders. May not even have known about the legend that had grown out of Nadine's death. The ghost who walked the woods.

"Actually," Nick said, "it's because of Ms. Hudson here. But I can't talk about official business. All I can say is that we both want to see Nadine get her justice."

He paused and Rachel could see that he'd been affected by the poem, too.

Then he said, "She's waited long enough."

Chapter Fourteen

The call from Charlie came shortly after dinner.

Late in the afternoon, Nick and Rachel showed up at cousin Thomas's house on Mosquito Lane, as requested. Thomas and his father had gone hunting the previous season and they still had some venison in the freezer.

Rachel had never eaten deer before. It had a slightly gamy taste that she wasn't used to, but she did her best to finish what she'd been served.

Thomas's entire family was crowded around the table, laughing and reminiscing about the summers Nick had spent on the reservation.

"Nick was a wild one," Thomas's wife, Remy, said. "I tried to get him to go out with me but he wasn't interested. I had to settle for Tom."

"Hey!" Thomas said, and they all laughed, the kids chiming in the loudest—a girl and two boys, ranging in age from six to ten.

Rachel felt welcome in their home, which radiated a kind of familial warmth she'd never experienced before. She was an only child and had felt a little lonely when she was growing up. She was close to her parents, but her father was always chasing a case and her mother had busied herself in community work that often kept her away from the house when Rachel got home from school.

Rachel was a latchkey kid and had learned to be self-sufficient. And while she wouldn't trade her life for anyone else's, there was a part of her that wished she'd had a family like this one to come home to every day.

In a place like this, too.

She could get used to living in Maine, she thought. With a family of her own. The beginning of which was growing inside her right now.

"So," Thomas said to her, "Nick tells me you're writing a book about him."

"He does, does he?"

She shot Nick a look and he threw his hands up in protest, frowning at his cousin.

"That isn't what I said."

"Why else would she want to hang around with a lug nut like you? Unless…"

Thomas looked from Nick to Rachel and back at

Nick again, then broke into a grin. "You been holdin'
out on me, bro. *Nice.* Very nice."

Rachel felt herself redden. She had nothing to be
embarrassed about, but there it was, so she blamed
it on the pregnancy.

Nick came to her rescue. "How about we change
the subject?"

"Good idea," Thomas said. "We wouldn't want
Remy here to get jealous."

Remy swatted him on the arm and they all laughed
again.

RACHEL AND REMY WERE sitting on the porch, watching Nick and Thomas toss a ball with the kids, when
Remy said, "I was serious, you know. I really did try
to get Nick to go out with me."

Rachel just looked at her.

"Don't get me wrong. Thomas is my soul mate and
I love him to death. He's a great husband and a terrific
father and I've never regretted a moment I've spent
with him. But Nick… Nick's got that extra something,
you know? Gets your motor running without even
trying." She smiled. "You made a good catch."

"Nobody's been caught just yet."

"Don't kid yourself. I've seen the way he looks
at you. You've got the hook in good." She nodded to
Rachel's belly. "And he'll make a great father, too."

What was this? Did *everyone* know she was pregnant?

Maybe it was time to buy some looser clothes.

They were silent as they watched the others play. Nick gently tossed the ball to the little girl, Chelsea. She fumbled it and it bounced off her shoe, rolling across the yard.

Nick ran to her and scooped her up, shouting, "Hurry, hurry! We can't let it get away!" as they raced after the ball, Chelsea giggling like crazy.

It was good to see Nick so relaxed. Good to see another side to him. And watching him interact with these kids made her realize that Remy was right. He *would* make a great father.

But it was way too early to be thinking about that.

Better to do what Nick had suggested and take it slow. Very slow.

The sun was almost down when Nick's cell phone rang. Rachel watched him take it from his pocket and put it to his ear, his expression darkening as he spoke.

Something had happened. She could tell by that look.

When he hung up, she got to her feet and went to him. "What is it? What's wrong?"

"That was Charlie," he said somberly. "Vern Robinson is dead."

"He didn't make it through surgery?"

"No, that's just it. The doctors said he did fine. A lot better than they expected. They even put him in his own room."

"So what happened?"

"Charlie went to the hospital to see him, see if maybe he was alert enough to answer a few questions. But when he got there, Vern wasn't in his room."

"What?"

"They found him in the trees outside the parking lot," Nick said. "Someone bashed his head in."

THEY ALMOST MISSED the last ferry.

The drive had been stalled by an accident on Bangor Road, and they pulled onto the dock only seconds before the gate went down.

The guy manning it didn't want to let them through, but Nick's uniform—and the look on his face—changed his mind.

A few minutes later, they were standing at the rail, staring out at the pale moon. Despite Charlie's bad news, Nick couldn't help thinking how breathtaking Rachel looked against the backdrop of the bay and the horizon beyond.

He marveled at the brain's ability to compartmentalize.

He pressed against her back, putting his arms around her waist. Mustering up his nerve, he finally decided to ask her the question that had been running through his mind ever since he found out she was pregnant.

"This is probably none of my business," he said.

She tensed slightly—a natural reaction to a statement like that—and he hesitated.

"I'm listening."

He ran his hands along the swell of her abdomen. "The father. Is he still in the picture?"

Rachel laughed.

"What's so funny?"

"If you talk to him, he's very much *not* in the picture. He thinks it's somebody else's baby."

Nick frowned. "That's a pretty insulting assumption. Who is this idiot?"

"My ex-husband, Dan. We jumped into marriage and pretended to love each other for four years, but it didn't take. We even tried to reconcile a few months ago."

He rubbed her abdomen again. "And this is your reward?"

"For me. But not for him. He has no interest in raising kids."

Nick shook his head. "He's a fool."

"Something else we can agree on."

"I'll never understand a man who doesn't welcome his own child into the world. *Any* child, for that matter. The Penawahpskewi cherish their young ones."

"I think most people do. Unfortunately, Dan's not most people." She turned to face him. "But you can see why I hesitate to get involved, can't you?"

"I'm not Dan."

"Believe me, I know that. But as funny as this may sound, neither was he four years ago. Things change. People change. And how can we know how we'll feel another four years from now? Another four months?"

Nick was silent, letting her words run through his head. Then he said, "You shouldn't do this to yourself, Rachel."

"What do you mean?"

"You can't keep punishing yourself for marrying a jerk. You have to move on. Be willing to take chances again."

"I guess I'm looking for the impossible," she said softly.

"Which is?"

"A guarantee."

He shook his head. "Nobody can give you that.

That's something you have find inside yourself. Trust your instincts."

"Believe me, I know. I think that's the problem. I keep second-guessing them." She paused. "I keep thinking about Nadine Orono's poem, too. She sounded so happy. So sure that her pain was finally gone. But look how she wound up."

"And look how Thomas and Remy wound up. We could go back and forth with this all night long."

"Then let's just leave it alone for now. You promised me you wouldn't push."

"You're right," he said. "The last thing I want to do is scare you away."

She smiled then and kissed his cheek. "Let's just concentrate on the moon for now."

Then she turned back to the rail and looked out at the sky.

Chapter Fifteen

The investigation was in full swing when they pulled up to the crime scene.

Charlie was crouched at the edge of the hospital parking lot with Bobbie Hooper, the department's lone forensics tech. They surrounded a numbered flag in the soil, right where Vern Robinson's body had been found.

Nick and Rachel approached them and Nick said, "What've you got?"

Charlie gestured. "Might be a footprint but we can't be sure."

"Looks like a partial," Bobbie said. "And judging by the size of it, I'd say it isn't fully grown. Probably a teenager."

Nick and Rachel looked at each other and Charlie caught the look.

"Can we talk a minute?" he said to Nick. "In private?"

"Sure."

Charlie got to his feet, then the two headed toward an ambulance that was parked about twenty yards away.

"What's on your mind?" Nick asked.

"Where the heck you been for the last five hours?"

"I told you. We went to question the victim's brother."

"And it took that long? What exactly is going on between you two, anyway?"

Nick frowned at him. "How is that any of your business?"

"We're in the middle of an investigation here, Nick. I know she's a hot little number and all, but I get the feeling you're letting your hormones take your head out of the game."

"What are you talking about? If it weren't for Rachel, we wouldn't even be looking into Nadine's death. We'd still be chasing some ridiculous ghost story."

"That's exactly what I'm saying."

Nick took half a step back.

"We can't be getting caught up in the past, Nick. People are dying, right here, right now."

"I realize that, Charlie. But like Rachel says—"

"Can we leave her out of it for a minute? She's a reporter. She has a different agenda than we do. She's looking for drama, we're looking for solutions. And I'm not the only one who feels this way."

"Burgess?"

Charlie didn't say anything.

"Since when do you talk to that idiot? I thought you hated the guy."

Charlie sighed. "I could live without him, believe me. But whether we like it or not, he's got some influence in this town and he could make life miserable for both of us."

Nick studied him. It wasn't like Charlie to be even slightly conciliatory toward Bill Burgess.

Then it hit him. "What did he promise you, Charlie?"

"What?"

"Did he come to you, try to make a deal? Tell you he'd make sure you got the top slot if you helped him squeeze me out?"

"It's not like that, Nick."

"Isn't it?"

Charlie slumped, lowered his head.

"Okay, it's true, he did come to me with an offer, but I told him to stuff it, all right? But if you'll pardon the expression, he's on the warpath and he wants you gone. He saw you and Rachel today, found out who she is, and he plans on using her as ammunition with the city council. Says you're too busy trying to get publicity to be effective as sheriff."

Nick felt his anger rising. "Where is he now?"

"I don't know. He was here a little while ago, saw what happened to Vern. I've got a feeling he's busy trying to round up the council for an emergency session, get you booted off the case."

Nick could barely control himself. He wasn't prone to violence but right now he felt like putting a fist in Burgess's face.

Charlie could apparently read minds. "Come on, now, settle down. Going after the guy will only make things worse."

"Any idea when this meeting's supposed to happen?"

Charlie shook his head. "I doubt it'll be tonight. Murders or no murders, I don't see anybody on the council interrupting their night of TV watching on Burgess's say-so. They're all probably half in the bag anyway."

Nick relaxed a little.

"All right," he said. "We can worry about him later. Right now I want you to get back to the office and run a database check on the name Little Bird."

Charlie frowned. "Little Bird? Is that some kind of tribal name?"

"I'm not sure," Nick said. "It could be, or it could just be a nickname."

"That's a pretty tall order. Where's this coming from?"

"A letter Nadine Orono sent to her brother shortly before she was murdered. She had a boyfriend. Called him Little Bird."

Charlie sighed again. "What did I just tell you? We've got more important things to do than wallow around in the—"

"Just do it," Nick said. "If the council cans my butt, you can take over and handle this investigation however you see fit. In the meantime, that's a direct order."

Nick didn't usually talk to Charlie like this, but his instincts told him that he and Rachel were on the right track and he needed Charlie to get on board.

"All right, fine," Charlie said. "But while I'm busy wasting my time, there's something I want you to think about."

Nick studied him warily. "What's that?"

"What I said at dinner last night might not have been too far from the truth."

Nick was at a loss. "Refresh my memory."

"That maybe we should consider that all these rumors are true. That what we're dealing with isn't human."

"You're kidding me, right?"

"I wish I were, Nick. But all those witnesses who heard Weeping Willow? Maybe they aren't as full of it as you think they are."

Nick squinted at him. "What are trying to tell me?"

"I left something out when I called you earlier. Something important."

"So don't keep me in suspense."

"I told you I came here to see if Vern was alert enough to be questioned, right? But when I went into his room, he was gone."

"Right," Nick said.

"But what I neglected to include was that as I was standing there wondering why Vern's bed was empty, I heard something coming from outside his window. It's what led me out here, straight to his body."

Nick had a feeling he knew what Charlie was about to say. "Go on."

"It was her, Nick. Weeping Willow. I heard her crying, plain as day." He paused. "So maybe you'd better think about that while you're busy making time with the cute reporter."

Then he walked off, heading to his cruiser.

RACHEL DROVE NICK TO HIS office, where he had left his car. She was exhausted and needed to get some sleep, but Nick planned to go back to the crime scene and figured he'd be there most of the night.

He'd told her what Charlie had said about Weeping Willow, and she didn't think Charlie would lie. And since she knew the possibility of a ghost being involved in this was slim to none, there was only one other direction to take it.

"Our killer enjoys taunting his victims," she said. "And he doesn't care who else knows it. In fact, he probably gets off on the idea."

Nick nodded. "I'm sure he gets some perverse satisfaction out of seeing everyone in town scared out of their wits."

"Maybe I was wrong about this whole Nadine thing. Maybe he's just using her as a means to an end."

"No," Nick said. "I think we're on the right track. These deaths are directly related to her murder."

"What about that footprint? Your tech seemed convinced it belonged to a teenager. Undoubtedly a girl."

"I'm betting the killer planted it, just to make the whole scenario more convincing. Really get people riled up."

"He seems to have Charlie convinced."

"Charlie's scared, too," Nick said. "He's the same

age as the other victims. He's probably wondering if he's on the killer's list."

"What's got *me* worried is that the killings are escalating. That's two deaths in only twenty-four hours."

"You don't have to remind me."

She pulled to a stop next to his cruiser. He popped open his door, then leaned over and kissed her on the cheek.

"Get some sleep," he said. "It's been a long day."

"Even longer for you, it looks like. When you're done at the hospital, come by my room. Maybe I can help you relax."

He grinned. "I appreciate the invitation, but you'll be fast asleep by the time I get back."

"I'm a light sleeper," she said.

"Good to know, but we wouldn't want Maddie to talk. And Lord knows she can talk."

Rachel laughed, squeezed his hand. "Kick some butt out there."

"I'll certainly try," he said.

As SHE CLIMBED OUT OF HER CAR at the Waterford Inn, she got that feeling again.

That she was being watched.

She turned, scanning the area, and saw no one. Maddie's neighbors were already inside their homes for the night. There were a few lit windows but most of them were dark and the street itself was empty.

Yet the feeling persisted.

Was someone standing in one of those darkened windows? Someone unfriendly?

Goose bumps worked their way up her neck and across her scalp as Rachel mounted the steps of the inn, fumbling with her key.

She got it into the lock, certain that there was someone standing directly behind her now, then the door was open and she slipped inside, closing and locking it as quickly as she could.

She let out the breath she was holding.

It's just paranoia, she told herself. *There's no one out there.*

Still, she parted the curtain in the doorway and looked out the glass at the shadows across the street.

The street was still empty.

Relieved but jittery, she moved across the foyer and through the archway, calling out as she went. "Maddie?"

No answer.

"Maddie? You still awake?"

It was nearing 11:00 p.m. and the poor woman had probably gone to bed. Her room was at the very back of the house, so maybe she didn't even hear Rachel.

Rachel started up the stairs, wondering if she should take a shower, but visions of scary movies started running through her head, so she decided against it.

Better safe than sorry, her father always said.

Instead, she'd follow Maddie's lead, and crawl straight into bed.

And maybe she'd sleep with the light on.

Chapter Sixteen

In the dream she was fifteen years old.

First day of school and she was walking down the hall, her footsteps echoing, her heart pounding. She was new here and afraid that she wouldn't fit in. Afraid that people would think she was different and would laugh at her.

Yet, oddly enough, there was no one here.

The hall was completely empty.

All the classroom doors hung wide and the rows of desks inside were unoccupied.

Where had everyone gone?

"You're too late," a voice said, the sound reverberating through the hallway.

Rachel wheeled around and saw Maddie on her hands and knees, scrubbing at a stain on the scuffed linoleum.

A stain that looked like blood.

"They've already come and gone," she said. "You'd

better get going, too. You don't want to be caught here alone."

"What happened?" Rachel asked, her eyes on the rag in Maddie's hand.

"I already told you. It was her. She won't rest until we're all dead."

"Nadine?"

"That's the one. The ghost who walks the woods."

"There's no such thing as ghosts," Rachel said. "It's all just a fairy tale."

Maddie laughed, kept wiping at that stain. "Tell that to Vern Robinson, or Caroline, or any of the others. Tell that to all the people who heard her out there in the trees. Like me. How do you explain all that?"

"I don't know but there has to be a rational explanation. The stories aren't true. Nadine was buried a long time ago and she's still in the ground."

"You think so, do you?"

"Yes."

Maddie looked up at her and smiled.

"Then tell me this, dearie." She lifted the hand holding the bloody rag, pointing a finger past Rachel's left shoulder. "Who's that right behind you?"

RACHEL WOKE WITH START, her heart pounding wildly.

The light atop the dresser shone in her eyes and it

took her a moment to realize that she was safely in bed, the blankets pulled up protectively around her, the nightmare nothing more than that.

As her heart slowed and she came fully awake, however, she heard a sound.

Faint. Muffled.

Coming from outside her bedroom window.

At first it didn't completely register in her brain. But then, with growing horror, she realized what it was.

A crying girl.

A soul in pain.

Nadine.

Throwing her blankets aside, Rachel got to her feet and went to the window. She fiddled with the latch, then pushed the window open.

There was no mistaking it. Nadine's sobs echoed in the night, carried across Maddie's backyard by the wind.

The moon was high, spilling its light across the wooded hillside, that ever-present mist gently swirling through the trees. The goose bumps that had plagued Rachel earlier were back again, doubling and tripling as cold fingers skittered up her spine.

She snatched her cell phone off the nightstand and scrolled through the menu. She found the voice memo app and clicked Record as she padded back to the window.

Holding up the phone, she aimed it toward the woods and the sound of Nadine's sobs.

Now she had proof that she wasn't dreaming. That the witnesses had been telling the truth.

Checking her clock, she saw that it was nearly 3:00 a.m. and she wondered if Nick was back from the crime scene. He needed to hear this right now.

She stopped the recording and tossed the cell phone on the mattress before charging into the hallway. Nadine's sobs were much fainter here, but still they echoed in the night.

Cold fingers continued to play along her spine.

The light from her room gave her just enough to see by. Down the hall, Nick's door was closed.

She went up to it, knocked. "Nick? Are you in there?"

She tried again. "Nick, wake up. It's Rachel."

Still nothing.

She checked the knob, it turned, and she pushed the door open. His bed was empty and still made. Just what she'd been afraid of.

Behind her, the crying abruptly stopped.

Hurrying back to her room, she went to the window but heard nothing. Even the wind was still.

What was going on out there?

Would they find another body tonight?

The stairs creaked behind her and she flinched. Froze. Turning now, she started back to her door, calling out as she went. "Nick?"

Silence.

"Maddie?"

She went into the hallway, looked toward the stairs, but there was no one there.

"Maddie?" she called again.

Feeling the sudden urge to get back inside her room and lock the door, she started to turn when something caught her eye—something she hadn't noticed before:

At the very end of the hall, the door across from Nick's was slightly ajar.

The room Caroline had stayed in.

Had it always been that way? She couldn't be sure. She'd been concentrating on waking Nick.

She knew she should listen to her gut and get back into her room, but something about that open door compelled her forward. As if the room itself was calling to her.

She knew this was just her natural curiosity at work, but the fact that the first victim had slept in that room the night she died was reason enough to check it out.

What would be the harm?

Still she hesitated, more movie scenarios running through her mind. Wasn't this usually the moment she'd be screaming at the screen, telling the heroine to turn back? That she was a fool for going inside?

After all, hearing Nadine's cries in the night was not exactly an indication that all was hunky-dory in the world. People died whenever they'd heard those cries.

Was she a potential victim, too?

No, she thought. She didn't fit the profile. And there were no killers in that room, just an open door. Nothing more, nothing less.

And nothing to be afraid of.

Besides, if anyone tried to attack her right now, she had enough adrenaline running through her veins to beat the snot out of him.

Pumping herself up, Rachel continued forward, but slowly. As she reached Caroline's door, she pushed it open and immediately found the light switch, flipping on the overhead light and bracing herself for whatever might come her way.

But nothing happened.

The room was empty except for the bed, a portable wardrobe closet and a small, low bookshelf that served as a nightstand with a small lamp atop it.

Maddie hadn't been lying about not cleaning the room. The bed was unmade and there was still remnants of fingerprint dust on the headboard, the dresser top, the lamp and bookshelf.

The bookshelf was nearly full, of course, books stacked neatly in two vertical rows, all hardbacks, most of them fiction.

Yet one of the books seemed out of place. It was larger and thinner than the others, its cover royal blue, with yellow typeface along the spine. It was laid horizontally across the top row of books, as if it had been stuck there by someone lying in bed.

Unless Rachel was mistaken, it was a high school yearbook. It was easy to miss. Nick and his team had probably assumed it belonged here. But it didn't. It didn't fit this room. Why would Maddie leave an old high school yearbook for her guests to read? That didn't make any sense.

So someone else had brought it.

Caroline?

Closing the door behind her, Rachel crossed to the shelf and crouched in front of it, scanning the spine.

Jefferson High.

The year printed below the words indicated that it was just over thirty years old.

A coincidence?

Rachel didn't think so.

Pulling it out, she flipped it open and found the

inside cover filled with the typical high school in-
scriptions in different colored pens. Lots of hearts
and flowers and promises to see each other next year,
full of sentiments like "Have a great summer!" and
"Miss you already!"

In the top left corner were the words *PROPERTY
OF CAROLINE KELLER.*

So Rachel had been right.

But now the question was *why*? Why would Caroline bring this book to Waterford Point with her? To
reminisce about old times?

Or was there something more to her trip here than
a meeting with a client?

Rachel began flipping through the pages, looking
at the fresh young faces that adorned them in living
black-and-white, her own high school memories filling her mind. Funny how so many people who had
meant so much to her back then were no longer part
of her life.

They'd all moved on. Moved away.

Waterford Point was a small town, however, and
Rachel didn't doubt that many of these students were
still in contact. They hung out on Saturdays mornings
with their kids at the soccer field, saw one another in
church on Sunday, at the diner and the dock, walking
along Main Street, waving and smiling at one another
as they passed.

Maybe not so much now. Now that there was killer out there. A killer who could be any of them, any of the faces in this book.

Rachel continued to flip through the pages and found *Keller, Caroline* in the Juniors section. A pretty blonde who probably never had any trouble attracting boys. Slightly upturned nose. Cute smile. Cheerleader. Honor roll student.

Rachel moved on, finding *Malone, Sheila*—victim number three. An outgoing senior. Another fresh face, but with a haunted gaze that seem to foreshadow the alcoholism that would plague her as an adult. Or had possibly already begun.

Next was *Penski, Ed*—victim two. Long-haired, a wispy, barely-there goatee. Also a senior. A bad boy from the looks of him, who probably spent a lot of time behind the band building playing cards and smoking cigarettes.

Rachel was flipping toward the back, looking for Russ Webber, when something fell from between the pages and fluttered to the floor.

She quickly retrieved it and discovered a faded photograph, the words *Wild Bunch* printed along the bottom border.

In the photo were several teenagers, cigarettes and beers in hand, sitting around a smoldering campfire, some of them unaware of the camera while others smiled or posed or flashed signs with their fingers.

There were six of them—three girls and three boys. Rachel immediately recognized two of the girls from their yearbook photos.

Caroline and Sheila.

And one of the boys was clearly Ed Penski.

She flipped the photo over, surprised to find more words on the back. The ink looked fresher here, written with a bold black marker:

I'LL TELL EVERYONE.

A chill ran through Rachel.

The killer had sent this to Caroline. Had probably lured her here with a threat of some kind.

Could he have been blackmailing her?

If so, for what?

What did he know?

Rachel flipped the photo over again and studied the faces. Caroline, Sheila, Ed. The others were a mystery to her. One of the boys looked as if he could be Vern Robinson, but the photo was faded and his head was turned to the side and it was hard to tell.

The third girl drew Rachel's attention now. Something familiar about her.

Needing more light, Rachel turned on the lamp

atop the bookshelf and held the photo directly under the bulb. As she looked at that third girl, it suddenly dawned on her who it was.

The girl looked much different here, which wasn't a surprise. All of the kids had gained weight and changed in appearance after thirty years. Rachel probably wouldn't have recognized any of them if it hadn't been for the yearbook pictures.

But there was no mistake.

She recognized the smile. The eyes.

It was Maddie.

She won't rest until we're all dead.

And with sudden horror, Rachel remembered the crying outside, and knew exactly what it meant. The killer was coming after Maddie now.

Tossing the yearbook and photo to the bed, Rachel jumped to her feet.

She had to get to her cell phone.

Call Nick.

And then she had to find Maddie.

Dread sluicing through her body, she quickly crossed the room and threw the door open—

—then froze in her tracks when she saw a large figure standing in the hallway, not two feet away.

A man with malevolent black eyes.

Emit Lattimore.

Chapter Seventeen

Before Rachel could react, Lattimore lunged and grabbed her by the throat.

"You think you can hide from me?" he hissed.

Rachel stumbled backward, her feet flying out beneath her, and he drove her onto the bed, his enormous hands squeezing the air out of her, his dark eyes shining with triumph.

In her mind, she was suddenly back in that interview room with Lattimore diving across the table at her.

He climbed on top of her now, applying more pressure with his hands. The room darkened as she gagged and choked, starting to lose consciousness.

Lattimore's voice seemed to be coming at her from a long, dark tunnel. "All I had to do was hack into your home computer, you stupid little witch, and there it all was—travel plans, hotel, dates, times, everything. You really need to be more—"

Rachel brought a knee up as fast and as hard as she could, nailing him between the legs.

Lattimore grunted and released her, staggering back, falling to one knee, breathing in great gasps.

"You little—"

Then she was off the bed and diving for the door. Lattimore swept an arm out. He got hold of her ankle and she fell forward, twisting as she went down, landing on her back. She kicked out at him, hitting him in the chest, and he flew back, his head slamming into the bookshelf.

The lamp atop it tumbled onto him, the lightbulb popping, and he batted it away, his face reddening, filling with fury.

"I'm gonna make you feel pain like you've never felt it before."

But before he could get to his feet, Rachel was out the door and running.

She hit the stairs, leaping down them two steps at a time. She could hear him behind her, crashing onto the stairway, but she didn't look back, didn't want to know how close he was.

Picking up speed, she reached the bottom of the steps and headed for the front door. Then he was on her again, grabbing hold of her shoulder, squeezing it with such force that pain rocketed through her.

She screamed, then spun and swung out, slamming

a fist into the side of his head. He lost his grip, stumbling sideways into the dining table. A chair toppled and he nearly went down again—

—but Rachel didn't waste any time. She ran for the kitchen, nearly slipping as she pushed through the doorway, her eyes scanning the room quickly until she spotted the cutlery block on the counter.

She grabbed the biggest, nastiest knife in the block, then darted for the side door, pushing her way onto Maddie's cement drive.

She headed for the street, running toward it in long, deep strides, her lungs on fire, her breathing ragged. As she neared the end of the drive, she heard a shout behind her and Lattimore was on her again, grabbing at her.

Rachel swung around, slicing the blade toward him, but it glanced off his shoulder and he just laughed, putting a palm against her face and shoving her toward the ground.

She stumbled and fell to her knees, the grit of the asphalt sending a thousand needles of pain up through her. She cried out, swinging the knife again, but he knocked it out of her hand and it clattered loudly on the cement.

He grabbed her by the chin, roughly tilting her face toward his. His own face was sweaty and he was breathing hard.

"You remind me of Alison," he said. "My second wife. She was a fighter, too. But I knocked the fight right out of her, just like I'm gonna knock it out of—"

A shot rang out.

Then a second.

A third.

All in quick succession.

Suddenly Lattimore's enormous hand was no longer clutching Rachel's chin and he was on the ground in front of her, gasping for air.

"You shot me," he wheezed, his dark eyes staring up at her in disbelief. "But you don't have a gun… How did you…"

Then the wind went out of him and his eyes glazed over, losing their light, as Emit Lattimore stopped breathing altogether.

The next thing Rachel knew, Nick was beside her, shoving his gun into his holster as he pulled her to her feet and took her into his arms.

"Are you all right?" he said. "Did he hurt you?"

"Oh, thank God," Rachel breathed, then fell against his chest and started to cry.

"So who the heck *is* this guy?" Charlie asked.

He and Nick were standing in Maddie's driveway, looking down at the body.

"You don't recognize him?"

"Should I?"

"Maybe you don't watch enough TV," Nick said. "This is Emit Lattimore. Guy whose wife disappeared without a trace a few months back. He's been all over the news ever since."

"I don't get it. What's he got to do with Rachel?"

Nick looked out past the driveway at the ambulance parked out front. Rachel was sitting inside, a paramedic checking her pupils with a light.

"She was pretty shook up, so I haven't had much of a chance to talk to her yet. All I managed to get out of her was that he's the subject of her latest book." He looked at the body again. "I guess he wasn't too thrilled about it."

"Doesn't much matter now," Charlie said. "At least she's got an ending."

Nick glared at him. "That isn't funny."

"Do you see me laughing? I gotta tell you, Nick, I'm starting to regret ever coming back to Waterford. The first few months were fine, but now I'm thinking this place is cursed."

"Don't start that again."

"I'm serious."

Nick looked at his deputy and could see that he was rattled.

Charlie was no stranger to police work. He had

done it for several years before returning to Waterford Point. But most of that work had been in towns even smaller than this one, little burgs that boasted no more than a couple thousand law-abiding citizens. The worst thing he'd ever had to deal with, he once told Nick, was a barroom fight that had ended in a stabbing.

Nick could see that the last few weeks were really starting to take their toll. And he knew he'd been wrong when he'd accused Charlie of wanting the top slot. The poor guy didn't look like he was much interested in being in law enforcement at all.

Not here, anyway.

"Charlie, tell you what. It's late, you're tired. Why don't you go home, get some sleep. Take a couple days off."

"What're you nuts? We're already short-handed as it is."

"We'll manage," Nick said.

Charlie started to protest but Nick held a hand up, cutting him off.

"I mean it, Charlie. I can see this is starting to get to you, and I need you in top…"

He paused, looking out toward the mouth of the driveway as a car pulled up and Bill Burgess got out.

Nick sighed.

Could this night get any worse?

Both he and Charlie braced themselves as Burgess spotted them and approached, looking down at the dead man, his eyes lit with excitement.

"Is it him? Is it our killer?"

"Sorry to disappoint you, Bill, but this guy doesn't have anything to do with the Weeping Willow case."

Burgess frowned. "Then who is he?"

Nick knew that this next bit of news wasn't likely to get a good reaction.

"Emit Lattimore," he said.

Burgess looked confused for a moment, then the realization crept into his eyes, followed by disbelief. "I don't get it. You mean the guy who's been all over cable news for the last six months? The one who disappeared his wife?"

"That's the one," Charlie said.

"But what's he doing here? Who shot him?" He looked at Nick. "Did *you* do this?"

Nick nodded.

"But why?"

Nick gestured to the ambulance. The paramedic was dabbing ointment on Rachel's injured knees.

"He attacked Rachel. Turns out she's writing a book about him."

Burgess gave Rachel a long, slow burn.

Then he said, "Do you realize what this means, you moron?"

Nick bristled. "I beg your pardon?"

"You stupid fool. Are you even remotely aware of what kind of media storm will hit this town the minute the news gets out?"

"We'll deal with it," Nick said.

"Deal with it? Yeah, you'll deal with it, all right. I'm sure you'll be quite happy to take the lead. I've been watching you, Chavaree. I know what kind of guy you are. How much you like being the hero. And now that the circus is coming to town, you can tell them all about how the big bad Injun tore Emit Lattimore a brand new—"

Nick decked him.

Burgess went down hard, grabbing at his nose as it started to spout blood, his butt hitting the asphalt.

Nick would have hit him again if Charlie hadn't held him back. "Easy, man. Easy."

Now Burgess stared up at him, his words coming out in nasally gasps. "You maniac… I think… I think you broke my nose."

Charlie said, "Get out of here, Burgess. Go home."

Burgess stared up at him, his eyes filling with tears.

"Go," Charlie said. "Now."

Burgess struggled a moment, then slowly got to his feet, a hand planted against his face as he stared accusingly at Nick. "I really think you broke it."

Nick shook his head in disgust. "I didn't even hit you that hard."

"Go home," Charlie repeated, still holding on to Nick. "Get your butt back in that car and drive, or I'll let him loose. You want that?"

Burgess looked at Nick with terror in his eyes, then stumbled back, moved quickly to his car, then paused as he was about to climb in.

"You're finished, Chavaree. Consider this your last night on the job. No way the board can keep you now."

Then he shut himself inside and drove away.

When he was gone, Charlie said, "It's been nice working with you, Sheriff."

Nick didn't feel even a twinge of regret. "He had it coming."

"Oh, I agree, and he'll get more than he deserves one of these days, but I don't think you need to be the one to give it to him. And after that little display, I think it's *you* who needs some rest."

Nick nodded, calmed himself down. "I guess we all do."

Charlie gestured to the body. "You know there'll be a formal inquiry about the shooting. And Burgess is right. If this guy's as famous as you say he is, we'll be inundated with news crews by tomorrow afternoon."

Nick shook his head. "How did things get so messy so quickly?"

"I hate to point fingers," Charlie said, then nodded toward the ambulance. "But it looks to me like your girlfriend has hurt us a lot more than she's helped."

Nick shot a look at him. "Don't even go there, Charlie."

Charlie threw his hands up. "I'm just sayin'. Things were a lot less complicated before she showed up."

Nick felt his anger rising again but he held back. Unlike Burgess, Charlie was a reasonable man, and he was only expressing an opinion. Even if it was dead wrong.

Nick did his best to let it wash over him. He was on edge and overly sensitive and there was no point in taking it out on anyone else.

Especially right now.

Rachel was finished with the paramedic and coming toward them, a look of grave concern on her face. He wondered if she'd seen what he'd done to Burgess.

"Are you okay?" he asked.

She nodded. "I checked out fine."

"What about the baby?"

"The baby's fine, too," she said hurriedly. "Have either of you seen Maddie?"

"Maddie?" Nick scanned the area. "I don't think so, why?"

He hadn't even thought about Maddie since he'd arrived. He'd been too busy blowing away bad guys and just assumed that she was around somewhere, poking her nose in everyone's business.

"I can't believe this," Rachel said, starting toward the house. "Everything happened so fast, I completely forgot about her."

"Rachel, what's going on?"

"No point checking in there," Charlie told her. "I did a sweep of the house when I got here to make sure your psycho friend didn't have any buddies hanging around. Maddie wasn't in her room. Come to think of it, I haven't seen her at all tonight."

Rachel stopped in her tracks, her expression morphing from worry to horror as she brought a hand to her mouth.

"Oh, my God," she murmured, tears springing to her eyes. "Oh, my God…"

Nick felt his gut tighten. "What is it, Rachel? Did something happen to her?"

"I heard the cries tonight. Outside my window. It was Weeping Willow."

"Weeping Willow?"

"Yes," Rachel said, then turned and started running toward the woods. "She has Maddie."

Chapter Eighteen

Charlie left to do another sweep of the house as Nick and two deputies caught up with Rachel. They crossed the yard into the woods, their flashlights blazing.

"Maddie?" Rachel called. "Maddie, are you out here? Call out if you can."

The only answer was the echo of her own voice.

She gestured to the flashlight on Nick's gun belt. "Give me your extra flashlight. We need to split up."

"No way," Nick said. "You've already been through enough. If the killer is out here…"

"I mean it, Nick. We don't have time to argue. I can handle myself."

"I might be inclined to believe that if I hadn't just put three bullets in a guy who was attacking you. We stay together."

"Look, just give me the flashlight. The more eyes we have out here, the better."

But Nick refused to budge.

She huffed at him and moved forward into the dark without a flashlight, and he came up close behind her, using his to light her path.

Rachel was frantic.

She could barely maintain her composure.

She didn't really know Maddie but she'd come to like her. Despite the woman's quirkiness, she was kind and unpretentious and always seemed to have a smile. And the thought that she'd been grabbed by the killer—or ghost, if Rachel was to believe what she'd heard outside her window—was almost too much to bear.

She won't rest until we're all dead.

The image of Maddie standing at the reception counter, using her scissors like a dagger, popped into Rachel's mind. She knew now that Maddie's words had hidden a very specific meaning. A meaning that went beyond a ghost story.

She won't rest until we're all dead.

Each of the victims was in the photograph Rachel had found, and Maddie must have known that sooner or later, it would be *her* turn.

But why hadn't she said anything?

She was living under the same roof as the sheriff, for godsakes. Did she think that this somehow made her safer? Even after what had happened to Caroline?

Or was the answer simpler than that?

Maddie had something to hide.

Just like the others.

"Over here!" a voice shouted, and Nick abruptly swung his flashlight to the right, shining it past a clearing toward a thick cluster of trees.

A deputy stood there with slumped shoulders, his own beam focused on a dark lump on the ground.

Rachel felt as if she'd been kicked in the gut.

They were too late.

Without waiting for Nick, she ran, crossing the clearing in ten easy strides, stopping short when she saw the face in the deputy's flashlight, her worst fears realized.

It was Maddie, looking like one of the dolls from Angela Webber's living room, her blue eyes glassy and staring heavenward, her forehead bloodied and bruised.

"Oh, God…" Rachel muttered. "If I hadn't forgotten about her."

"You don't know that," Nick said.

He was standing beside her now, panting from the run. He crossed to Maddie's body and pressed his fingers against her neck, feeling for a pulse, but it was obvious by his expression that he wasn't getting one.

"She could've been dead before you came home," he told Rachel. He spoke softly, his voice cracking, and Rachel saw grief creeping into his eyes.

"I'm so sorry," Rachel said softly. "I'm so sorry…"

"So what now?" Charlie asked.

They were standing in front of the inn, assessing the crowd of neighbors that had gathered to gawk and point.

"I think we'd both better start looking for new jobs," Nick said. "Maddie's death pretty much sealed our fate."

"Mine, maybe. But you were already fish food the moment you decked Burgess."

"True. But I have to admit I enjoyed it."

Charlie raised his eyebrows. "Well, well, Sheriff, maybe there's hope for you, after all."

"Maybe." He shook his head. "I'll tell you, Charlie…seeing Maddie like that… That just strengthened my resolve to find this creep."

"Maybe you'll get lucky before they take your badge and gun. Or before he runs out of victims. But I'm not banking on it. We don't even have a suspect."

"Speaking of which, did you ever check into that name I asked you about? Little Bird?"

Charlie nodded. "Just about every database in the known universe. And here's what I got."

He reached into his shirt pocket, and when he pulled his hand out, his fingers formed a zero.

"Now, if you don't mind, I'm gonna take you up on your offer and go home, go to bed and try to resist the urge to put a gun in my mouth." He smiled. "Then I'll start making travel plans."

Doffing an imaginary cap, he crossed to his cruiser, climbed inside and drove away.

NICK FOUND RACHEL IN THE ROOM that Caroline had stayed in, surprised to see her curled up on the unmade bed.

Her gaze was fixed on the wall, her cell phone clutched tightly in one hand. She stirred as he stepped inside. "Rachel?"

She looked up at him, her eyes glistening. "Maddie's dead because of me, Nick."

"That's nonsense. You couldn't have known this would happen."

"Couldn't I?"

"I don't see how."

She pulled herself upright. "I told you what I heard tonight. If I hadn't let myself get distracted—"

"You were *attacked*, Rachel. You had a few things on your mind."

"Maybe I wouldn't have if I hadn't gone after Lattimore in the first place."

Nick sat down on the bed, ran his hand along the back of her calf. "You can play the blame game forever," he said, "but that still doesn't mean it's your fault." He noticed a small bruise on her ankle. "How did you get involved with that maniac anyway?"

She sighed. "How else? I go where the story is. And sometimes it finds *me*."

"But why try to kill you?"

"I made him angry," she said. "Something I could easily have avoided if I hadn't gone after him so hard. I violated my own rule, Nick. I prejudged Lattimore and forgot to maintain my objectivity." He noticed a subtle shift in her eyes, a look of regret that went well beyond what had happened here tonight. "Just like I forgot with you."

"Don't say that."

She shook her head. "I don't know. I don't know what I mean. Everything's upside down. I just want to curl up into a ball and make the world go away."

He put an arm around her, pulled her toward him and stroked her shoulder. She rested her head against his chest and started to cry, and for that moment he knew exactly how she felt. Making the world go away was just what they needed right now. Both of them.

They stayed that way for a while, Rachel's tears staining his shirt. Then she flinched and touched her stomach, surprise in her voice. "Oh, my God…"

"What's wrong?"

"The baby. She moved. That's the first time."

"She probably senses you're upset," Nick said, then lowered his hand, pressing it against the subtle swell of her abdomen, feeling a faint stirring inside her.

Feeling life there.

"Maybe this will help."

He hummed softly, a lullaby his mother used to sing to him whenever he was sad, and the baby immediately began to calm.

"There, you see? I think I have a fan."

Rachel looked up at him and smiled. To his relief, the regret he'd seen there earlier had disappeared.

"More than one," she told him. "More than one."

Then she kissed him.

A FEW MOMENTS LATER, Rachel said, "There's something I think you need to listen to."

She held out her cell phone and Nick just stared at it. "I don't understand."

"I set it to voice memo mode. Just press the green button and listen."

Nick took the phone from her, wondering what this was about, then found the button and pressed it. The speaker came alive with the faint but unmistakable sound of someone crying.

A girl.

A ghost?

"This can't be real," he said. "It has to be a trick." He looked at Rachel. "You're not turning into Charlie, are you? Starting to believe the ghost story?"

She took the phone back and shut it off. "I'm a little too practical for that. But this recording is proof that the killer enjoys taunting his victims. And I think I may know why."

"I'm all ears."

Rachel scooted to the side of the bed, then reached for a book on the bookshelf next to it. What looked like a yearbook. Opening the cover, she slipped out a photograph and handed it to him, facedown.

There were words printed across the back in bold black ink:

I'LL TELL EVERYONE.

Nick flipped the photo over and saw a faded image of several teenage kids sitting around a smoldering campfire, the words *Wild Bunch* written in the margin below.

"Where did you get this?"

"It was Caroline's. She brought it with her."

Nick flipped the photo over again and reread the words on the back. "Some kind of blackmail scheme?"

"That's what I thought at first, but now I'm convinced this was really just a way to lure Caroline home again. So he could kill her."

"Okay, but the question is still why?"

She nodded. "That's what I've been trying to figure out all along. How these people are connected and why someone would want them dead."

"And?"

"I think I was right about it relating to Nadine Orono's murder, but I also think I got it backward."

"How so?"

"I said they were probably all witnesses, remember?"

Nick nodded.

"But if they saw Nadine get killed all those years ago, why wouldn't they just go to the police? And why didn't Maddie ever tell you about it? Especially after the people she used to hang out with started dying?"

"Because she didn't want anyone to know."

"Exactly," Rachel said. "None of them did. They were the Wild Bunch, their own secret little club. A club whose members went on to battle depression, alcoholism…guilt."

Nick processed what she was saying and suddenly understood. "They weren't witnesses to Nadine's murder. They were the perpetrators."

"They killed her, Nick. Her and her foster parents. Then they tried to cover up what they'd done and they've been covering ever since."

"That may all be true," Nick said, "but it still doesn't explain who's killing them all off."

"Maybe he's in that photograph."

He looked at the photo again. It was so faded it was almost useless, yet when he studied it carefully, the faces did begin to look familiar. Especially Maddie's.

To think she'd had something to do with Nadine's death just didn't compute. She'd always seemed so kind. Cheerful.

But then people have their own ways of coping, don't they? They suppress and deny and pretty soon that awful memory becomes little more than a bad dream, hidden by a smile.

Rachel said, "I've matched all the faces in that photograph to the victims. All but one. The lone member of the Wild Bunch who's still alive."

She scooted over close to him now and fingered the boy at the center, a snarky, superior smile on the kid's face, a cigarette dangling between his lips.

He looked to be the leader of the group. The baddest of the bad boys, and girls, in this case.

Nick squinted at the image, trying to get the face to register. And as the realization of who it was spread through him, he couldn't quite believe what he was seeing.

A little over an hour ago, he had bloodied this creep's middle-aged nose.

"It's Bill Burgess," he said softly.

Chapter Nineteen

They couldn't get to Nick's cruiser fast enough.

As he started the engine, Nick pulled out his cell phone and dialed Charlie's number.

It rang several times before Charlie picked up.

"I was just about to climb into bed," he said. "Don't tell me we have another body."

"No, but we do have a suspect."

"*What?* Who?"

"Bill Burgess," Nick told him.

"Burgess? What are you, nuts? I know he's a pretty sad specimen, but I don't take him for a—"

"Just trust me," Nick said. "I can't explain right now. Round up the troops and get your butt over to his house. I'll meet you there in fifteen minutes."

He hung up and turned to Rachel. "Charlie's a skeptic for once. He doesn't think Burgess has it in him."

"I would've said the same thing about Maddie."

Nick nodded. "Good point."

BILL BURGESS'S HOUSE was in Chaser's Ridge, not that far from the burnt-out shell that Nadine Orono and her foster parents had once called home.

Imagine having a reminder like *that* in your neighborhood.

Rachel hung on to the cruiser's hand brace as Nick tore up the hill like a madman. A few minutes later, they pulled into Burgess's driveway.

The house was big and sprawling in all of its New England splendor. The kind of place that suited a mayor and former judge. It spoke of money, but didn't shout it.

Nick had told Rachel that Burgess lived alone, after a nasty divorce several years back. His ex-wife had found him so unbearable that she'd moved out of Waterford Point altogether.

Did she know she was living with a killer?

Burgess's car was parked near the front door and Nick pulled up alongside it. The moment he killed the engine, however, they heard a now all-too-familiar sound—

The echo of a girl crying.

Even with the windows up, it was clear, coming from somewhere in back of Burgess's house. Somewhere in the trees.

Dread stirred in Rachel's stomach. She and Nick

exchanged glances, then Nick gestured toward the front door. It was ajar.

The sight of it brought on a feeling of déjà vu.

"Maybe Charlie was right," Nick said. "Maybe we're wrong about Burgess. He could be a victim, too."

"There's one way to find out."

Rachel was about to open her door when Nick reached over and grabbed her by the elbow.

"You've had enough excitement for one night. And so has the baby. I'll do this alone."

His concern for the baby heartened her just as the lullaby had, but she needed to be part of this.

"I'll be fine," she told him.

"Rachel, I mean it. I don't want you going in there. I'm not willing to take the risk that you get hurt again. Either of you."

He moved his hand to her belly now, stroking it, and she felt herself melting under his touch, reluctantly giving into his demand.

"Consider this a onetime thing," she said, then locked herself in.

"Keep an eye out for Charlie and the crew."

Then he was out his own door and running toward the house.

TEN MINUTES WENT BY.

Rachel sat and listened to Nadine's mournful

sobs, which went on and on without a rest. Without mercy.

Charlie and the others still hadn't arrived and she was starting to wonder if this was all just another bad dream. Any minute now she'd see Maddie on the porch, wiping up blood, asking her, "What's that behind you?"

Without meaning to, Rachel turned and glanced into the backseat. Released a breath.

All clear.

She checked the clock on the dash. Had too much time passed?

And where the heck was Charlie?

Calm down, kiddo. They're on the way. They'll be here before you know it.

She'd brought the yearbook and the photograph with her, and decided to distract herself by studying the photo again. Pulling it out, she looked down at a seventeen-year-old Bill Burgess, staring into the camera with that snide, petulant look on his face.

She hadn't been in the same room with him for more than five minutes, but she didn't think he'd changed all that much. If he was the killer, she doubted he felt much remorse.

But as she stared at the photograph, a thought suddenly occurred to her. Something she'd missed.

Stupidly. And now that she realized it, she couldn't believe just how stupid she'd been.

She had wrongly assumed that Burgess was the last of the victims and had been cutting down his old classmates in order to keep them silent about what they'd all done.

But there was someone unaccounted for in this picture. Someone she and Nick had neglected to include, and if you took just a moment to think about it, it was as obvious as can be.

The person behind the camera. The one who *took* the photo.

Was it another member of the Wild Bunch?

Rachel pulled the yearbook into her lap, opened it and began searching through the pages, hoping to find another photograph of this bunch, one that would include the missing photographer.

But when she got to the "Random Shots" section, which featured various photos of campus life, nothing on the pages jumped out at her.

Until she came to the last photograph.

It wasn't a shot of the Wild Bunch, but a black-and white photo taken inside of a classroom, facing a row of desks, all of them empty but one.

A young, dark-haired girl sat alone, staring forlornly at the camera, her unhappiness clear.

Rachel read the caption: *Nadine Orono.*

The sight was heartbreaking, and the last lines of the poor girl's poem instantly ran through Rachel's mind:

I never knew what joy could be
Until that fateful day
He came to me on silver wings
And took my pain away.

But it wasn't Nadine's image that held Rachel's attention. Instead, her gaze shifted to the one other person in the photo—

A young boy, well in the background, on his way out of the classroom. He stood frozen in motion in the doorway, an old-school boom box in his hand, his head turned, his gaze squarely on Nadine.

And it was obvious, even in this small photo, that he cared for her. Deeply.

It was Little Bird.

Rachel didn't have any trouble recognizing the face this time. The name printed next to Nadine's confirmed it:

Charlie "Bird" Tevis.

Chapter Twenty

The house was as still as a tomb.

Rachel shut the door behind her and felt the urge to find a light switch. But she resisted. Instead she flicked on the extra flashlight she'd found in Nick's trunk.

Shining it in front of her, she moved through the foyer, the polished wooden floorboards creaking beneath her feet as she stepped under an archway into a large, expensively furnished living room.

She knew by its design that the house was old, but it had been completely refurbished and, as far as she could tell in this light, it was meticulously clean.

Nadine's sobs continued to echo outside. There was a kitchen off to Rachel's right and the sound seemed to be coming from that direction.

She crossed to the doorway and paused when she reached the threshold, her heart kicking up a notch as her flashlight beam hit the smooth kitchen tiles.

There were drops of blood on the floor.

She thought of her dream again, and Maddie's warning, and goose bumps rose on the back of her neck. She quickly turned to see if someone behind her.

But the living room was empty.

Turning back to the kitchen, she moved closer to the blood. It glistened in the light.

Fresh.

And there was enough of it to assume that someone was badly hurt.

Nick?

Nadine's sobs continued outside, as if running on an endless loop. Rachel was about to cross to the doorway leading into the back yard when her flashlight beam caught something else—

A small, dark shape laying on the tile near the refrigerator. A gun.

Nick's gun.

Rachel's heart thumped faster.

No, she thought. *No, please… Let him be all right. Let him be safe.*

Overcome by urgency, she moved quickly to the door, threw it open and peered outside, past a rustic-looking deck with a gas barbecue grill.

There was a wide expanse of lawn beyond it, and

those ever-present trees she had come to fear, and the mist clinging to them.

Nadine's sobs beckoned to her.

She wanted to call Nick's name, but if he was out there, he wasn't alone. Calling out would only draw attention to her.

The wind began to rise, whispering in the trees like a cold, sinister voice, underscoring Nadine's endless sobs.

Rachel trembled, no longer fully convinced that there wasn't something otherworldly out there. Something that had risen from the grave and was looking for revenge.

But no. She couldn't allow herself to think that.

It was Charlie. Charlie was doing this. He had to be. Didn't he?

Steeling herself, she started across the lawn toward the sound, stopping midway when she got that feeling again.

That she was being watched.

Something moved at the periphery of her vision. She swiveled her head to the left and saw a shadow in the mist, darting through the trees.

Fear shot through her and she flicked off the light, quickly flattening herself on the grass. She lay there for a long moment, watching the trees intently, but the only thing that moved was the mist, swirling like smoke in the wind as Nadine's sobs continued unabated.

Come on, Rachel. Pull yourself together.

She hesitated, then slowly got to her feet again, each step an effort as she moved to the edge of the lawn, stopping just short of the first line of trees.

Using Nadine's sobs as her compass, Rachel made her way through the trees, determined to find the source of the sound, to prove to herself that it was nothing more than a ruse. A trick.

Then, to her surprise, the fog parted slightly and there was just enough moonlight to see it, sitting on a small boulder near one of the trees.

A battered old-school boom box.

The very same boom box that Charlie Tevis had been carrying in the yearbook photograph.

Nadine's sobs rose from the speakers—not a ghost, but a simple tape recording.

Rachel felt an uncontrollable rage overcome her.

Moving quickly to the boulder, she raised her flashlight and brought it down hard, smashing it against the boom box, again and again, the cheap plastic splintering beneath it until the sobs abruptly stopped, leaving only the whisper of the wind.

Once again getting that feeling that she was being watched, she spun around to find a dark figure sitting on the ground behind her.

He stared at her wide-eyed, his back against a tree, his wrists bound, mouth gagged.

It was Bill Burgess. Alive but frightened out of his wits. And lying there on the ground next to him was Nick.

Oh, my God, Rachel thought, rushing to Nick's side. The first thing she saw was the blood on his forehead. Dread washed through her as she frantically turned him upright, thinking for one horrible moment that he must be dead.

Then he moaned, softly, his eyes flickering open— dazed but alive.

Thank you, Lord. Thank you.

Pulling him upright, she threw her arms around him, hugging him with everything she had. Whatever doubts had plagued her over these last hours—doubts about her feelings, about their chances together— vanished in that instant. And she knew that if they got out of this alive, she would stay with him forever.

"How touching."

Rachel jerked her head around and saw Charlie Tevis behind her, still in his uniform, his pistol in his hand.

He pointed it at her.

"I really didn't want it to come to this," he said. "But when Nick called me and told me to check into Little Bird, I knew it was only a matter of time before

someone remembered that 'Bird' was my nickname
in high school. So I had to work fast. Escalate my
plan."

Burgess moaned and Charlie shot him a warning
glance. He stepped toward them now. Rachel kept
her eyes on that gun.

"You see, I loved Nadine Orono. More than you
could possibly imagine. The first time I saw her, I
thought she must be the most beautiful creature I'd
ever laid eyes on." His gaze hardened. "Unfortunately, my friends didn't see it. Especially good old
Burgess here. Isn't that right, Billy Boy?"

He moved up to Burgess and kicked the sole of his
left shoe. Burgess's eyes went wide and he moaned
again.

"You see, we were all buds back then. Me, Billy
Boy, Batty Maddie, Caroline, Russ. We were off the
radar as far as everyone else was concerned. Bunch
of pathetic misfits who thought we were something
special."

He waved his gun at Burgess. "Billy considered
himself the leader of our little group, and he had
a long history of being a hater. Especially Native
Americans. Waterford Point has always had its fair
share, and they were worth less than spit to him.
And Nadine was no exception." He nodded to Nick.

"Nick's had a taste of what that feels like, haven't you, partner?"

Nick said nothing, but Rachel could see that his eyes had cleared slightly and that was a good sign.

"So asking Nadine to be part of the Wild Bunch was out of the question. She and I started sneaking around, spending a lot of time together. I think for the first time in that poor girl's life, she was happy.

"Then it all went sour. One day Billy and the others got drunk and caught me and Nadine making out in the woods. Burgess here about popped his cork, started roughing us up, and pretty soon the others joined in.

"I don't remember exactly how it happened, but the next thing I knew, Nadine was on the ground, her head bleeding, and it pretty obvious she'd never get up again.

"But the cover-up was much worse than the crime. My good buddies, my friends, my compadres decided to take Nadine's body back to her house. Vern Robinson's big idea. They attacked the Culbersons, doused the place with some gasoline they found in a shed outside, then set it on fire."

Charlie went away for a moment inside his head. "The worst part of all is that I swore I'd turn them in. Every single one of them. But then Burgess here pulled me aside and said if I breathed a word of any of it, he'd tell the cops that it was all *my* idea, and before the day was done, my own family would wind up just like Nadine's." He kicked at Burgess again. "And I caved, didn't I, Billy Boy? Folded right there in front of all of you. Too scared of my own shadow to say boo.

"Our little group broke up after that. But nobody ever said a word. Not one word. My family and I moved away, but I had dreams every single night about Nadine. Heard her crying. Calling to me for help. And when I ran into an old neighbor of mine and heard the story of Weeping Willow... Well, I knew it was finally time to act. I wanted these people, these so-called friends of mine, to feel the fear that Nadine felt. To know that she was out there, exacting her revenge." He smiled. "So here we stand."

Rachel knew he wasn't looking for questions but the writer inside her had to ask just one.

"I don't understand," she said. "If they all knew you were back in town, didn't they suspect you were the one?"

"Maybe. Probably. But what could they do? If they said anything, they knew they'd only reveal themselves for what they really were. A bunch of murderous cowards.

"Good old Billy here even came to me, all in a tizzy, accusing me flat out. But I turned the tables on him. Told him he was next on my list and the only way he'd stay alive was to help me. We even tag-teamed on Russ Webber. You see, Billy isn't all that much without a gang to back him up. Isn't that right, Billy Boy?"

Burgess moaned again, fire in his eyes.

"Anyway," Charlie said, "it was good to get that off my chest but I've wasted enough breath. It's time to finish things up."

"What do you plan to do with us?" Rachel asked. She still had the flashlight in her hand and gripped it tighter.

"Nothing you're gonna like, believe me. By the time the sun comes up, you, Nick and Billy here will all be facedown in the burnt-out rubble of the mayor's house. Then I'll go up to Nadine's place and put a bullet in my own head. Maybe get a chance to see her again."

Smoke billowed at from the back door of the house behind him. Taking a quick glance at it, he said, "Guess those timers work just like advertised."

"You're out of your mind," Rachel told him.

"You know, you may be right about that." He moved toward her now, gesturing with the gun. "But I'm not so far gone I didn't notice you've got a flashlight in your hand. So I'd suggest you drop it, sweetie, or I'll have to shoot your friend Nick."

Rachel sucked in a breath, loosening her grip, but not completely releasing the flashlight.

"Come on, now," Charlie said. "I really don't want to pull the—"

Suddenly Burgess sprang to his feet and lunged toward Charlie with a muffled scream.

Charlie spun and fired, cutting him down—

But the distraction gave Rachel just enough time to move. She leapt at Charlie and swung the flashlight, smacking it into his forehead. He cried out in pain and stumbled back, grabbing at his head.

Rachel didn't wait around to see how badly she'd hurt him. Taking Nick by the arm, she helped him to his feet, urging him to run. They moved together through the trees, heading toward Burgess's house.

They were nearing the edge of the woods when shots rang out. Nick, who seemed to have finally regained his senses, grabbed Rachel's arm and yanked her to the side, bullets punching the ground around them.

He urged her toward a clump of trees.

"What are you doing?" she whispered. "You're hurt. We have to get to the car."

"Charlie's an expert shot, remember? We step foot on that lawn and light or no light, he'll take us out."

"And you think staying here is any better?"

"I have an idea," Nick said. "And he's just loony enough, he may fall for it."

"Fall for what?"

"Give me your cell phone. I got a plan."

CHARLIE TEVIS WAS LIVID. He couldn't believe he'd let Rachel get one over on him like that. If it hadn't been for that fool Burgess, his plan would nearly be finished, and by sunup he'd be standing in the shell of Nadine's house, ready to join her once and for all.

He cursed Nick for ever bringing that meddler in on this case. If it hadn't been for her, he could have continued to take his time, doled out punishment on his own schedule, working the town that didn't care into a frenzy over the ghost of the Weeping Willow. Let them feel the anguish he'd felt for the last thirty years.

But Rachel had ruined all that. And when he got her and Nick in his sights again, he'd be sure to take her down first.

Let Nick watch her die.

He knew they were hiding somewhere but it wouldn't be long before they made a wrong move. And when that happened he'd show them just how good a sharpshooter he really...

Charlie paused as he heard a sound, not too far away.

Was that what he thought it was?

It was barely loud enough to be discernible, but if he wasn't mistaken—

It was Nadine. Crying.

But how could that be? He'd seen Rachel destroy his boom box, smashing the cassette inside it—the cassette he had recorded all those years ago when he and Nadine first started seeing each other.

He'd been something of an audio buff at the time and he'd had this crazy notion that he'd get her story on tape. Get her to talk about her family and her culture. But the moment he started the recorder up and asked his first question, she had burst into tears, throwing herself against him and sobbing uncontrollably.

It was that moment, and those tears, that made Charlie realize just how much he was in love with her.

But if Rachel had destroyed the cassette and the boom box, how could it be playing now?

Unless…

Unless…

It really *was* Nadine.

Had she come back to him?

Charlie didn't waste any time. He started running

through the trees, moving toward the sound, calling out to her, "Nadine! I'm coming Nadine!"

But when he reached a clearing, he came to an abrupt stop, his gaze focusing on a spot in the center. And there, lying on the ground, was a cell phone, the sound of Nadine's sobs rising from its speaker.

And as disappointment nearly overwhelmed him, he felt pressure in his back and froze.

"Drop the gun, Charlie, or I'll drop you."

It was Nick. Pressing a gun against him.

Or was he?

Charlie knew for certain that Nick had dropped his own pistol when Charlie had hijacked him in the kitchen. And if Rachel had a gun, she would have used it on him instead of that flashlight.

Which meant he was bluffing.

But Charlie wasn't a scared teenager anymore. And in *his* mind, bluffs were meant to be called.

NICK KNEW HE WAS TAKING a pretty big chance with what had to be the oldest trick in the book—poking a stick against the small of Charlie's back—but desperate people take desperate measures.

Unfortunately, Charlie wasn't stupid.

And despite his size, he was a pretty agile guy. Without warning, he spun around and pointed his gun at Nick's chest.

But Nick threw his hand out, knocking Charlie's arm to the side as the gun went off, the shot going wild. Nick swung again, knocking the weapon from his hand.

Charlie lunged at him, driving him back toward a tree. Nick's head slammed against it and pain rocketed through his skull.

The world tilted sideways as Charlie came at him again, grabbing his shirt. Nick swung out blindly, knocking him back, but his head was pounding now and he was quickly losing strength.

Then Charlie kicked a foot out, tripping Nick up and Nick went down to the dirt like a sack of cement, the world spinning wildly around him.

He heard Charlie huffing for breath, then the shuffle of shoes against earth as his deputy moved across the clearing, looking for his gun. A moment later, he found it and moved back toward Nick. There were two of him now, overlapping in Nick's vision.

"The funny thing is," Charlie said. "I really do like you, partner. It's a shame to see you go this way."

Then he raised the gun and put his finger against the trigger.

And that's when Rachel beaned him with a fallen tree branch, knocking him out cold.

Gluskabe felling the monster frog.

A moment later, she was helping Nick to his feet

and pulling him into her arms. And as the warmth of her embrace enveloped him, Nick's only thought was that he didn't need to die to go to heaven.

He'd already found it right here.

Epilogue

By the time the ferry reached the dock, Rachel was feeling a little queasy.

She still didn't travel well on water, and the sandwich she'd eaten at the train station was starting to back up on her. This time, however, she couldn't blame it on pregnancy.

As the ferry gate opened, she moved with the handful of homeward-bound commuters and rolled her suitcase onto the dock, looking out toward the village. Waterford Point looked the same as always, but at least it was quieter now.

"Welcome back, missy." It was Walter, the old fisherman who manned the gate. "How was your conference?"

"Same as always," Rachel told him, "big, loud and crowded."

"You sell any books?"

"I *signed* quite a few, I'll tell you that."

"Well," Walter said, "ever since you published that thing, everybody and his grandma wants to come to town. You've made us famous, young lady."

Rachel smiled. "I do what I can."

A year and a half had passed since that night in the woods. It turned out that Bill Burgess's wounds weren't fatal, and thirty years after the death of a young, innocent Native American girl, one of her killers went on trial, convicted in part because of the testimony of Charlie Tevis.

Charlie himself was doing life without parole for his killing spree in Waterford Point. Rachel sat through both trials, taking notes and structuring a narrative. By the time it was over, she had a brand-new book to publish, calling it *The Ghost Who Walked the Woods*.

It was her most personal book to date, and her fifth bestseller.

"You take care now," Walter said. "Tell Nick hello for me."

"Will do," Rachel told him, then rolled her suitcase toward the parking lot.

As she came around the corner, she saw Nick waiting by the car, their year-old bundle of heaven squirming in his arms, happy to see her mommy.

Rachel kissed them both and the baby squealed in delight.

Their daughter was born without incident and Nick had been there for the delivery, had cut the umbilical cord himself. And over the next several months he'd proven to be every bit the wonderful father Rachel had hoped he'd be.

With her mother and father and Nick's cousin Thomas and his family in attendance, they had married in a small ceremony, promising to have and hold forever, a promise Rachel had no doubt they'd both keep.

And anytime they thought back on those terrible days and nights in Waterford Point, they simply had to look at their little girl and remember the joy in the world.

She was the most beautiful creature Rachel had ever seen.

They called her Nadine.

* * * * *

Harlequin
INTRIGUE

COMING NEXT MONTH

Available May 10, 2011

#1275 BABY BOOTCAMP
Daddy Corps
Mallory Kane

#1276 BRANDED
Whitehorse, Montana: Chisholm Cattle Company
B.J. Daniels

#1277 DAMAGED
Colby Agency: The New Equalizers
Debra Webb

#1278 THE MAN FROM GOSSAMER RIDGE
Cooper Justice: Cold Case Investigation
Paula Graves

#1279 UNFORGETTABLE
Cassie Miles

#1280 BEAR CLAW CONSPIRACY
Bear Claw Creek Crime Lab
Jessica Andersen

You can find more information on upcoming
Harlequin® titles, free excerpts and more at
www.HarlequinInsideRomance.com.

HICNM0411

REQUEST YOUR FREE BOOKS!
2 FREE NOVELS PLUS 2 FREE GIFTS!

Harlequin

INTRIGUE

BREATHTAKING ROMANTIC SUSPENSE

YES! Please send me 2 FREE Harlequin Intrigue® novels and my 2 FREE gifts (gifts are worth about \$10). After receiving them, if I don't wish to receive any more books, I can return the shipping statement marked "cancel." If I don't cancel, I will receive 6 brand-new novels every month and be billed just \$4.24 per book in the U.S. or \$4.99 per book in Canada. That's a saving of at least 15% off the cover price! It's quite a bargain! Shipping and handling is just 50¢ per book in the U.S. and 75¢ per book in Canada.* I understand that accepting the 2 free books and gifts places me under no obligation to buy anything. I can always return a shipment and cancel at any time. Even if I never buy another book, the two free books and gifts are mine to keep forever.

182/382 HDN FC5H

Name	(PLEASE PRINT)
Address	Apt. #
City	State/Prov.	Zip/Postal Code

Signature (if under 18, a parent or guardian must sign)

Mail to the **Reader Service:**
IN U.S.A.: P.O. Box 1867, Buffalo, NY 14240-1867
IN CANADA: P.O. Box 609, Fort Erie, Ontario L2A 5X3

Not valid for current subscribers to Harlequin Intrigue books.

**Are you a subscriber to Harlequin Intrigue books
and want to receive the larger-print edition?
Call 1-800-873-8635 or visit www.ReaderService.com.**

* Terms and prices subject to change without notice. Prices do not include applicable taxes. Sales tax applicable in N.Y. Canadian residents will be charged applicable taxes. Offer not valid in Quebec. This offer is limited to one order per household. All orders subject to credit approval. Credit or debit balances in a customer's account(s) may be offset by any other outstanding balance owed by or to the customer. Please allow 4 to 6 weeks for delivery. Offer available while quantities last.

Your Privacy—The Reader Service is committed to protecting your privacy. Our Privacy Policy is available online at www.ReaderService.com or upon request from the Reader Service.

We make a portion of our mailing list available to reputable third parties that offer products we believe may interest you. If you prefer that we not exchange your name with third parties, or if you wish to clarify or modify your communication preferences, please visit us at www.ReaderService.com/consumerchoice or write to us at Reader Service Preference Service, P.O. Box 9062, Buffalo, NY 14269. Include your complete name and address.

HII1

*With an evil force hell-bent on destruction,
two enemies must unite to find a truth that turns
all-too-personal when passions collide.*

*Enjoy a sneak peek in Jenna Kernan's next installment
in her original* TRACKER *series, GHOST STALKER,
available in May, only from Harlequin Nocturne.*

"**W**ho are you?" he snarled.

Jessie lifted her chin. "Your better."

His smile was cold. "Such arrogance could only come from a Niyanoka."

She nodded. "Why are you here?"

"I don't know." He glanced about her room. "I asked the birds to take me to a healer."

"And they have done so. Is that *all* you asked?"

"No. To lead them away from my friends." His eyes fluttered and she saw them roll over white.

Jessie straightened, preparing to flee, but he roused himself and mastered the momentary weakness. His eyes snapped open, locking on her.

Her heart hammered as she inched back.

"Lead who away?" she whispered, suddenly afraid of the answer.

"The ghosts. Nagi sent them to attack me so I would bring them to her."

The wolf must be deranged because Nagi did not send ghosts to attack living creatures. He captured the evil ones after their death if they refused to walk the Way of Souls, forcing them to face judgment.

"Her? The healer you seek is also female?"

"Michaela. She's Niyanoka, like you. The last Seer of Souls and Nagi wants her dead."

Jessie fell back to her seat on the carpet as the possibility of this ricocheted in her brain. Could it be true?

"Why should I believe you?" But she knew why. His black aura, the part that said he had been touched by death. Only a ghost could do that. But it made no sense.

Why would Nagi hunt one of her people and why would a Skinwalker want to protect her? She had been trained from birth to hate the Skinwalkers, to consider them a threat.

His intent blue eyes pinned her. Jessie felt her mouth go dry as she considered the impossible. Could the trickster be speaking the truth? Great Mystery, what evil was this?

She stared in astonishment. There was only one way to find her answers. But she had never even met a Skinwalker before and so did not even know if they dreamed.

But if he dreamed, she would have her chance to learn the truth.

Look for GHOST STALKER by Jenna Kernan, available May only from Harlequin Nocturne, wherever books and ebooks are sold.

HNEXP0511